FIONA PARTRIDGE is a therapist and teacher.

Having always been a boo spent nose deep in a book. Sh library at home!

The Colour of Marriage: Annie's Story is Fi's second book after the runaway success of her debut novel *The Colour of Marriage*.

For more information and all the latest news on Fi, please visit www.fionapartridge.co.uk

ALSO BY FIONA PARTRIDGE

The Colour of Marriage

For more information on Fiona Partridge and her books, visit:

www.fionapartridge.co.uk
www.silverwoodbooks.co.uk

The
Colour
of
Marriage

ANNIE'S STORY

FIONA
PARTRIDGE

SilverWood

Published in 2022 by SilverWood Books

SilverWood Books Ltd
14 Small Street, Bristol, BS1 1DE, United Kingdom
www.silverwoodbooks.co.uk

ISBN 978-1-80042-205-6 (paperback)
ISBN 978-1-80042-206-3 (ebook)

British Library Cataloguing in Publication Data
A CIP catalogue record for this book is
available from the British Library

Page design and typesetting by SilverWood Books

To my beautiful little mess maker, Charlotte.

Never stop making mess, my Angel. I love you more!

Your Momma

xxxxx

Daz

For your unwavering support.

I'll get you some more biscuits as a thank you.

Wifey

xx

Acknowledgements

To Daz, thank you for once again putting up with me asking "is that a word?!!" I do love you!

To my Mum and Dad, thank you for never wavering support, encouragement and constant need to know when the books are being published!

Oh, and hopefully by the time this one is released, Dad will have read the first book!

Jenn and Mollie, for so many things I can't even begin to write them all down, so I'll just say I loves you mind!!!

And finally thank you to you for wanting to hear Annie's story. I sincerely hope that some of Ann's wise words strike a chord with each of you – she's a wise bird that one!

Don't forget to visit my website and tell me what you think. www.fionapartridge.co.uk

Enjoy!

Fi

xxx

Lawson,

Turns out this is my journey with Cancer, also my hopes for you and the kids should I not win this fight.

But know that I will fight till my last breath because I love you all so very much.

Your Ann

xx

So, I started this journal / diary?? to give me a space to express my thoughts, feelings and worries. out it's a road map as I navigate my journey with cancer. At times I'm writing to myself – my past self and my future self. To you Lawson. But mostly I'm trying to find some sense of the unfathomable.

But it's more than that. It's my hope for you and the kids should I not win this battle.

But please know I will fight to my very last breath to stay with you, because I love you. I know I've already said that!!

I love you with my every fibre and I don't want to leave you.

All my love always to you all-ways.

Mommy
and
Annie
xxxxx

Friday 25 March

Today is D Day, literally! Diagnosis Day.

I've got an appointment with Dr Pacey at 10.40am – the surgery phoned me last night to make an emergency appointment for today as the doctor wants to see me as soon as possible.

That doesn't sound good, does it? I'm sitting here in the conservatory now with the house still asleep; all I can hear is Beau's snoring and the boiler clicking on to warm the house before everyone wakes up. As I listen to the creaking pipes I scold myself yet again – I wish I'd gone to the doctor sooner.

For the surgery to ring me and get me back in so soon after the blood tests on Wednesday has only confirmed my fear there is something seriously wrong.

Maybe it's an inner knowing? A sixth sense? I can't seem to put it into words, but I just know.

There's always that niggling voice in the back of your head that pain means something awful! Bloody voices in your head are always throwing negativity at you. Why can they never utter the winning lottery numbers?

The exhaustion has been worse over the past week, and

that's what really pushed me to go and see the GP; I couldn't brush it off as just the day-to-day impact of running a home and looking after our two children.

Right, then. Time to get everyone up and start this day, no matter what comes my way.

~

It's just past 9.25pm. The kids are finally both in bed and asleep. Lawson is still at work and I'm alone in our bed.

Today didn't quite go as planned.

When I entered Dr Pacey's consulting room, another person was sitting next to him, a middle-aged woman who looked like she would make a great aunty to someone.

Her name is Dr Tanya Prescott. She is a consultant and had come into the surgery especially to be at my appointment today.

I've always found Dr Pacey such a kind soul. He takes time to listen to people's worries, concerns, and dramas and then calmly steers them in the right direction.

"Annie, thank you for coming in so quickly. We've had the first of the blood tests back. It's not the news we'd hoped for, I'm afraid. Early indications are that you are suffering with pancreatic cancer." Dr Pacey looked awful – just awful. "Dr Prescott is here to talk to you about what we've found so far, and what's going to happen now."

I moved my gaze to Dr Prescott, who was sitting next to the kind man; what the heck had he just said?

14

The doctor cleared her throat. "Annie, I've reviewed the initial blood tests we've had back. Please know that not all the results are in at the moment from the scan you had on Wednesday. As Michael said, I can tell you that it is pancreatic cancer T4b N2 M1. What this means is, T for the size of the tumour – very large. N, has it spread to the Lymph nodes? Yes. M, has the cancer spread beyond the main site? Yes. All of this is just medical jargon, Annie. What we need to focus on is simply S4 – stage 4 secondary cancer. It's terminal, Annie. I'm so sorry."

I know I sat there staring open-mouthed, flicking my gaze between the two people before me. Thank God for the body's intuitive ability to breathe. Indeed, they had the wrong person? They were reading someone else's records. Yes, that's it, there's been a mistake – a very terrible mistake!

No. There's no mistake.

Licking my lips, trying to return some moisture to my mouth, I looked at my hands in my lap. I wasn't shaking; I was still.

Looking at them again, I took a deep breath and simply asked, "How long?"

"That's a tough question to answer, Annie. There are a lot of variables, different factors – no one can say for certain," said Dr Prescott.

"HOW LONG?" I said again with more urgency.

The two doctors exchanged a look. "Six weeks maximum. I'm so sorry," Dr Prescott answered in a quiet tone. She did look like she meant she was sorry that she'd just told me I'd got six weeks left to live.

What a terrible thing to have to tell people that their days are coming to an end. How do you leave that kind of interaction at the office and not take it home with you?

Huh! It's funny being told you've only got weeks to live. I didn't get angry or even sad. I felt like I wasn't even in the room.

"We can try a new drug," Dr Prescott went on. "It does have side effects that can become quite consuming. But the initial trials in Europe have been very promising. Extension to life has been increased by as much as 12 months."

"What will happen to me as I reach the end? Symptoms I mean?" I managed to ask.

"Well, that depends on the route you choose to take. With no medication? That's very hard to tell, Annie, as we will have to battle the disease's natural progression. Sickness, tiredness, loss of appetite." The doctor listed these off on her fingers. "Potentially, hair loss, incontinence, confusion, and skin pigment could change. It won't be pretty, Annie, it won't be pretty at all. I'm advising you to let all the people around you know that you are sick – you're going to need their help."

I stood up and thanked both doctors for their time and kind words and promised to think about everything they had said. Dr Pacey said he'd ring me on Monday as he guided me to the door of his consultation room.

Picking up Lexie and Louis helped me focus. Something is comforting about the structure children bring to your time. Having a treat of a fried chicken takeaway for tea enabled me not to give the diagnosis another thought until now, as I sit in bed.

Do I want meds………..? No, I don't think so.

Do I want to live………..? HELL YEAH! But meds could extend the length of time I've got?

Do I want to tell Lawson…….? My gut says no, but I don't know why? I have to tell Mum and Dad though.

Will it win……..? Honestly? I don't know, but I'll give it a bloody good fight.

Telling Lawson is a given, isn't it? Why the doubt…?

Why the heck am I hesitating???????

I admit our relationship isn't at its best at the moment.

NO that's an outright lie – it's bloody shocking!

I'm going to need him now more than ever. The children are going to need him.

Yet it's been like we've drifted apart; our paths are moving away rather than meandering side by side.

I need my husband.

Do I feel any different internally knowing there is a disease eating away at my body?

Actually no!

Mentally I'm exhausted.

But internally I really don't feel any different to this

morning. I don't have a flashy sign about my head saying, 'ticking time bomb' or 'cancergirl'!

Outwardly there's no appearance of what I've been told is going on inside.

Huh!

Interesting.

Can I feel cancer?

No, I can't – just the side effects.

Huh (again!).

I'm tired, but I doubt sleep will come easily.

Saturday 26 March

Nope, sleep didn't come at all last night. Lawson came home around 10:00pm, showered and went straight to sleep, he never even attempted to see I was awake.

I know I can't avoid the gorge-sized hole that has developed between us in recent months. I've just felt so rough at times that all my energy has gone into just functioning.

I gave up trying to fall asleep at about 12.30am. I grabbed a blanket from the back of the sofa in the conservatory and wrapped it around my shoulders and sat on the loungers in the garden with Beau curled up next to me.

I let the tears fall hour after hour. Sobs racked my diseased and dying body, thoughts and emotions washed – NO, crashed – across me throughout the night, as I felt hard done by. Angry. Frustrated. Confused. Scared. Worried. Mostly I felt sad. Sad within my very soul, as the reality of my journey set in.

At 6am I showered, and put my face on and began to make breakfast for the hungry hounds. I woke them both with breakfast in bed. They loved it. My nanny's homemade pancake recipe never fails to win over folks.

Lawson was still sound asleep. He missed a memory-making time.

I dropped the kids with Janey as planned. Nan Janey is a firm favourite, along with her gigantic chocolate box that Lawson and I aren't allowed anywhere near. Then I took a slow and steady drive over to Mum and Dad's. I knew they'd be at home even though my visit was unannounced.

Mum ushered me in with such enthusiasm that I wasn't sure I'd be able to break her happiness. But I did. I told them.

"I need to tell you both something." I managed to find the strength, staring down at my half-empty cup of tea, which I placed on the coffee table.

"Ok, darling," said Mum, as she fluffed the cushions behind her on the sofa.

"You know I haven't been feeling great over the past few weeks? Well, I went for a scan last week and had some blood taken earlier this week." They both looked at me, shock crossing their faces.

"Ann, you never said. Mum would have come with you to the appointment."

"Yes, of course I would, darling." Mum agreed with Dad.

"I know. I got called to the doctor's surgery yesterday," I said, looking down at my hands. I took a deep breath. "I am dying." I looked up and stared into their eyes as the shock turned to confusion, back to shock, and then they realised what I was saying.

"I've got pancreatic cancer!" Wow, that was easier than I thought it would be – saying it out loud. "The long and short of it, from what the doctor said, is that I haven't got long – six weeks, maybe a little more."

My strength failed me, and the flood gates crashed open: "What am I going to do?"

They both cried, held me, cried, held me, cried again, held each other. They asked questions, some of which I simply couldn't answer mainly because I hadn't even thought of them myself!

Funerals?

End of days?

Flowers?

Cremation?

Burial?

The kids?

Rob?

Mostly, however, there is the stark realisation that I hadn't even considered how my diagnosis, my cancer, would impact those around me.

I feel powerless right now. I've no idea how it must feel to be experiencing it without it actually happening to you, to witness your loved one dying?

I now realise how selfish I'd been last night and this morning when I only thought of myself. This wasn't just happening to me. I don't think cancer ever just happens to the patient, does it?

~

My two little bundles of distraction came home around 5pm and Janey stayed for tea with us three. Lawson was hunkered down in the home office as per usual. He didn't even come out to say hello to his mum!

Never one to miss anything (ever), Janey gave me a big hug as I showed her out. "Is everything ok, love?" she said as she nodded her head in the direction of the office.

"Oh yes, everything is fine," was all I managed to say. It wasn't quite a lie, but neither was it quite the truth.

'Fine' – such a great word, offering the recipient the opportunity to fill in as desired.

Vocalising that my marriage was crumbling was more complicated than saying my body was crumbling. That would mean acknowledging the elephant in the room.

One elephant at a time, thanks!

I already feel like I'm failing everyone by not being able to be well. I can't admit I've failed in what I promised would be a colourful marriage.

"How's he getting on at work? I tried to call him earlier this week, but he didn't pick up or ring back!"

"Oh, Janey, you know he's never been great at answering his phone! Always on silent, isn't it?" I tried to laugh and make light of the situation. "He's doing well at work; they seem to be very busy."

"That's good to hear." She hugged me again. "If you need

22

me, just ring," she whispered into my ear.

Lawson still hasn't come to bed, but I can hear him chuckling – he does love watching comedies on the TV.

Mum just texted:

Goodnight my baby girl. Please know how truly loved you are, and we will support you whatever you decided to do. Me and Daddy will be beside you every single step of the way. I was the first to love and I will always love you. Mum x

I know I'm going – that's a very difficult concept to accept. The hard bit to accept is that I don't want to leave; I don't want to break my mummy's heart.

It's 5.05am and I'm sitting up, leaning against the headboard. My bedside lamp is on low. Lawson is asleep, sprawled on his back next to me, snoring his head off!

I'm in a lot of pain, and it woke me up. When I went to the loo, I caught my reflection in the mirror – God, I look awful!

I just need to keep a lid on 'Hector' for as long as I can.

Oooh, I've decided to call the cancer Hector. Cancer sounds like you're a doomed soul. Hector sounds like an old eccentric uncle who likes exploring and brings you random gifts and sherbet lemons!!!!

I'm staring down at Lawson. The pain isn't the only thing keeping me awake. I keep looking at him, and wondering why I've not told him yet.

I've thought about telling him more than I've actually thought about dying. I just don't know if I have the strength to witness breaking his heart.

Why, though, can't I tell my husband the most important information of my life?

The answer that keeps coming back is that I want the time

24

I have left to be 'normal'. I do not want him to look at me with pity, with sadness. I've done it – when someone has told me that they have cancer, I've looked at them with pity. Almost like they are doomed! It's just human nature. Not intended to be malicious or to treat the person differently – you just can't help it.

I want Louis and Lex to hug me because they want to, not because they don't know how much longer they've got me for.

As their mommy, that's my job. As long as there is breath in my body, I will always do the worrying for my babies.

I've given much thought to what Dr Prescott and Dr Pacey said to me on Friday about accessing drugs that will potentially extend my time. But I don't want to deal with all the possible side effects – the list is a plethora of horribleness. I'm going to ring the GP surgery tomorrow and tell Dr Pacey my decision.

I feel within my very soul that I will be able to manage the ongoing impact of Hector rather than start to fight an unknown quantity of possible side effects.

My beautiful family will not suffer any more than needed because of me. I will try my hardest to ensure their world is filled with colour each day.

~

The gap between Lawson and me is so wide right now that it's almost easier to continue being distant than summoning the energy and being the first to start moving back together.

Is that weak? Am I being selfish?

I tried to hug him in the kitchen earlier, but he just moved out of my arms and started talking to Lex.

I've done this. I take complete and total responsibility for the state of my marriage at the moment.

My distance and overriding need to protect the three of them has created this wall.

Have I made a mistake? There isn't a manual you can refer to once Hector gets hold of you. You must make hard decisions that will ultimately impact your remaining days and those who love you and the days they will live without you being there.

Have I boxed myself in, when all I want to happen is for Lawson to hold me tight so that I won't break?

~

I spent an immense amount of energy (that I don't have!!!!) on dinner today – roast beef. I hoped my true, unconditional love would emanate from the Yorkie pud. Everyone seemed to love it – even Louis asked for seconds!

I've come to bed alone. I can hear Lawson laughing – he's talking, so he must be on the phone. He must be talking to Zak – I hope it's Zak?

GOD!

WHAT??

I've just had to stop writing.

I've had endless thoughts go through my head, that it could be another woman he's talking to.

NEVER EVER have I ever questioned Lawson's loyalty in all our years together.

What the hell is the matter with me!

Hector is screwing with me, every bloody aspect of me. I've never been jealous.

Is it not enough that it's going to take my life? Why does it have to take my sanity and belief?

AGGGGGHHHHHHH FOR FUCK SAKE!!!!!!!!!!!!!!!!

Good grief – now I'm bloody swearing!

I wouldn't blame Lawson, you know, if…

If he has found another woman.

I just had to stop writing again, pull myself together and wait for the tears to stop flowing.

God that possibility hurts, but I've not exactly been the best wife over the past few months. Lately I've barely let him touch me, not because I don't want him to, but because I've been uncomfortable, in pain and lacking energy.

Maybe I'm damaging us by not telling him?

It's hard sitting here facing death square in the eyes. But it's harder facing the real possibility that my husband doesn't want me anymore.

When I stood at the altar in front of a church packed with our friends and family and declared my vows all those years ago, I knew I would be with Lawson until my last breath. I had hoped he felt the same – has he changed his mind? Has my distance changed his mind?

Monday 28 March

Today, I feel, is going to be a struggle. Right now, I'm so glad I agreed to give up my job when Louis came along and stayed at home to look after both kids. There is no way I could have battled Hector, looked after the house and our babies, and worked.

I've got to keep a positive mindset. I like to keep my energies high. But there is a wave of pure fear that keeps trying to edge closer and threatens to engulf me.

Last night, while soaking my aching muscles under the bubbles of a warm bath, I read that actively acknowledging the negativity is a positive thing to do. It sounds a bit bizarre, but according to experts, it works.

I suppose that's a bit like what I'm doing with this journal. I'm writing what I'm thinking and feeling, therefore releasing any attached emotion to it.

One expert said to be creative with your negativity, create jigsaws or drawings, even crosswords. So here goes:

C	A	C	S	T	I	V	S
K	A	W	K	S	L	S	C
N	L	N	L	A	L	S	A
H	O	A	C	D	B	O	R
F	N	B	A	E	A	L	E
T	E	R	H	A	R	U	D
P	K	O	P	T	J	K	W
A	S	S	K	H	L	P	A
I	R	N	Q	C	R	D	B
N	S	T	M	D	A	F	E
C	M	R	L	Y	G	O	H
L	E	A	V	I	N	G	M
D	U	E	S	N	Y	H	I
A	Z	F	S	G	T	K	J

Cancer	Leaving	Alone	Dark
Ill	Dying	Scared	Loss
Death	Pain	Fear	

Hopefully, the negativity being present but jumbled up among the other letters will allow the impact to be lessened.

I'm going for my monthly reiki treatment soon and that always makes me feel so much better.

For years I've sworn by my monthly session. When I gave up work, it was one of my conditions – that I must still get to keep the reiki treatments, as I can't do without it. Lawson says it's all voodoo magic – I say it's simply bloody magic.

I left a message with the GP surgery for Dr Pacey this morning, telling him I'm not going down the medication route, and that I'm not going to tell Lawson what's going on.

~

Dr Prescott called me this afternoon to confirm that she had received the message through Dr Pacey and that she will be personally taking over my clinical care, with Dr Pacey picking up everything else.

She advised me again to reconsider telling my loved ones, as I'm going to need them. However, at the moment I'm doing ok.

After taking some pain killers before dropping the kids off at school and nursery, the waves of pain that were sweeping over me subsided.

I went to my favourite place – The Boat Shack. I really enjoy it there – it allows me time to think, and it's a great treat for the kids.

I know my time with my children and Lawson is going to be

shorter than I'd ever hoped, so I need to make sure each day counts.

I've always been an organised bod, but now I feel it's even more important – I do love a good list! So, I made a to-do list of things that I need to get done.

To do before I leave

1. Write Louis and Lexie birthday cards for each year, up to their 21st

2. Write Christmas cards to the kids, Lawson, Mum and Dad and Andy until the kids reach their 21st year. Oh, and Janey

3. Write individual letters to Lou, Lex, Lawson, Mum and Dad, Andy and Zak

4. Buy presents for the children for birthdays and Christmases – money? Mum and Dad might be able to help

5. Support for the children? Any organisations?

6. Support for Lawson? Zak?

7. Organise my funeral. Lawson doesn't need to do that

8. Sort out all my papers and get rid of everything that's old

9. Prepare something for Lawson to find when I've gone, explaining what has been happening – perhaps more than a goodbye letter?

I've just texted Mum:

I'm making a list of things I'd like to get done before...
You know... I'd like to buy, and wrap presents for the
kids' birthdays and Christmases for the coming years.
Could you help me?

She replied almost instantly:

*Of course. Of course, darling. How about me and you
make a day of it? I'll drive and we'll go to the shopping
village. We can even have some lunch and me and
Dad will pay for it all? You don't need to worry about
anything, my girl. I love you.*

I sobbed silently as I read Mum's reply. God, my wonderful
mum always had a way of sweeping me and my brother up to
snuggle us better when we were little, and now she's doing that
all over again.

Knowing Mum and Dad are able to help me financially
is such a relief. I'll make sure that they get every penny back,
once...

Giving up my job was never a hard decision I've always
wanted to be a momma and to have the option to stay at home
and devote my life to them was easy. Missing my pay packet,
however, was tough at times. The money Lawson gives me is

more than enough for the household needs and my personal stuff. But it's not enough for such a big hit.

Poor Mum and Dad – when I told them what was happening, they asked if I'd tell Andy. Of course, I will. My wonderful, amazing, ridiculous, funny, smart, handsome brother whom I love with a passion.

He's just bought his first home, alone, and I'm due to go over and see it next week, armed with a packet of his favourite biscuits. I even offered to unpack a few boxes. I told Mum and Dad I'd talk to him then.

There was a time when it was just the four of us, the Stephens Clan, as Dad called us, and we had such a happy childhood, filled with laughter and happiness. Then along came Lawson and everything changed for the better, but I'm so grateful for those childhood days. I always look back and smile. Summer holidays in Brixham, South Devon, ice cream from Tim's local van for a Sunday treat. Having our first swing and slide set for Christmas and both of us insisting we weren't in the least bit cold and could therefore spend all of Christmas morning playing on it, multiple jumpers included. We were both like blocks of ice but didn't dare admit it! Oh! Oh! Sharing a room for six weeks while Dad decorated Andy's room – six long, laughter-filled nights.

I know many siblings who say they bickered and fought while growing up, but Andy and I never did – well, other than who got to sit in the front seat of the car, but that's everyone, right?

The fleeting thought I had last night that Lawson wasn't talking to Zak keeps trying to become more prominent and not so fleeting. I still believe he is the most handsome man I've ever seen. Those deep blue eyes – like oceans, his mop of unruly chestnut hair, that smile! Oh, that smile has made my heart flutter more times than I'd care to count. He is my soulmate, of that I'm sure. That same smile has been passed to Lou and Lex and it's beautiful.

I cannot break their hearts. I do not want whatever time I have left with them to be tainted with sadness, sorrow, what-ifs, or even pity. I will not do that to them.

Every minute counts now.

This evening I made sure that dinner was filled with laughter as we made our own pizzas, which was so much fun. I was crying with laughter and Louis was sporting a rather fetching tomato sauce moustache, and melted cheese down his top again!!!

Lawson missed a great night.

He misses out on so many fun times by being at work.

Tuesday 29 March

The pain is manageable this morning. I'm trying to only take the strong pain meds Dr Prescott prescribed when I absolutely need them. They make me slower and the only way I can describe it is that they make the world seem to be at arm's length.

I'm meeting Liv for a coffee this morning, then off to the GP's for more blood tests to monitor my levels. Dr Prescott has said that this will now be a weekly thing as she wants to keep a close eye on me.

I have no idea what time Lawson got in last night. I managed to get a good night's sleep, and I feel the benefit of that today. I'm uncomfortable, but I feel ok. He'd already gone to work when I woke up with my alarm just now. He works so hard and I'm so grateful that he's able to provide for our family, but I haven't spoken to him since yesterday morning – my heart aches.

So, I'm going to pull on my big-girl pants and grow up. I'm going to get up, get showered and dressed, wake my babies, and begin our day. But first I'm going to text him:

Miss you.

Hopefully I'll get a response.

~

Liv was her usual bubbly self. She was so excited to tell me that she and Zak are trying for a baby – they'll make amazing parents. I am so happy for them, but there is an undercurrent that is tinged with sadness because I know I'll never get to meet their baby; I'll never get to hold him or her. I'm going to miss so much. So much that in any normal circumstance, I now recognise, I would have just taken for granted.

I happened to mention in passing how nice it is that the boys still laugh together after all these years, how it's nice to hear it like on Sunday night.

"Sunday night? I don't think Lawson was talking to Zak on Sunday night. We always have a ban on Sunday evenings. We both turn our mobiles off before we have dinner and don't turn them on again until Monday morning – we always have done. But you know what, Ann, you're right. They are really good for each other."

I felt something physically sink inside me when she said that. Lawson wasn't talking to Zak on Sunday night. That annoying little voice inside my head was right. Question was, who was he talking too? And more importantly do I want to know?

Time to go and collect the mess makers from school. I don't

think I'll get time to ponder on this for much longer; my two herberts tend to have a way of consuming me completely.

~

Lawson came home tonight before the kids were in bed, which was lovely and a rarity these days.

Although I quickly found out he wasn't staying! He'd come home to shower and change his clothes because he was 'wining and dining' a potential new client at the Turntable Hotel on the outskirts of Worcester.

Thankfully he was still home to kiss the kids goodnight, and they were both so happy to have daddycuddles before going to sleep.

I pulled Lexie's door closed a little – "Not all the way, Mommy!" and I whispered, "Of course baby, we need to let the dreams in, don't we?"

I love my children so much that it hurts. Somewhere deep inside me is a growing ache, knowing that with each passing day I'm drawing closer to the time that I'll have to leave them.

I was just about to go downstairs and tidy up before a soak in a hot bath when I saw Lawson putting on his best shirt and tie in our bedroom. I walked up behind to help him get his tie right.

I don't know! Maybe I'm reading too much into it, but I could have sworn he stiffened against my touch, almost pulling away slightly.

But I kept those big-girl pants on and turned him around

to face me so I could straighten the tie and pull the collar down, staring at him face-to-face – the only man I've ever truly loved.

Holding his collar in both my hands so he couldn't pull away, I moved in slightly and cautiously kissed him gently, just brushing his lips.

Softly, unsure. I've never ever been unsure about kissing Lawson before – ever. It felt like an un-walked path, and I needed to tread lightly. It felt like he wasn't going to respond. I began to pull away, sadness beginning to swell in my stomach.

No! This is _my_ husband.

Being braver than I felt, I pushed back into the kiss and moved my arms up and around his neck, as a small moan escaped from his lips.

He slid his arms around my back and manoeuvred me towards the bed. This was the man I'd married, the man I loved, the man who owned my soul.

"I've missed you. Don't go away from me," I whispered into his ear as he climbed on top of me.

He froze – literally! Stared at me then climbed back off the bed, straightened his tie and said, "I'll be late if I don't leave now." Then he walked out!!!

Just like that!

I was left with my dress hoisted up around my waist and lying diagonally across the bed.

I cried hard into my pillow. I sobbed about how worthless and useless I felt, how much I love and miss my husband, how powerless I was, and how much I love my children. I cried for how much I wanted to live.

I'm losing him. I now see that, as I'm sitting in bed, all cried out, but I don't know how to stop it. I don't know if I have the energy to stop it. I don't know if I have time to stop it.

Why are relationships so flipping difficult?

Wednesday 30 March

I feel like utter hell!

The kids are at school and nursery. I'm not sure how I managed to get both where they are meant to be and on time – oh and fed!

I've come back home, and I crawled up to the shower and lay on the floor of the shower cubicle – clothes and all – and allowed the warm water to penetrate into my bones. I just lay there, and after what felt like an eternity I stripped off and washed my body, climbed into some fresh clothes and snuggled down under the duvet and here I'll stay until it's time to collect the kids again.

~

My plan to stay snuggled under the covers didn't go as planned.

The pain in my torso was so bad I texted Mum:

Please come

She did and took over everything.

Thursday 31 March

BLEUGH!!!!!!

Where's the takeaway pizza menu???????

Friday 1 April

Mum and Janey are lifesavers.

Mum took over on Wednesday when the pain was too much. She called Dr Pacey and he came out to adjust my pain medication. It took till last night for them to start to work.

Mum organised for the kids to go to Janey's house after school yesterday for tea, so thankfully I only had to feed myself, and I was hungry. The leftover pizza was calling my name, I could hear it – leftover pizza for breakfast, once the kids are safely deposited at school, then I'll tell you more.

~

God, I needed that! I feel so much better this morning. I spoke to Dr Prescott late yesterday afternoon and she said it's probable that these bouts of pain will come in waves and knock me off my feet. She said, to put it plainly, it's cancer, moving and spreading throughout my body.

She offered again to send over details of local hospices that can help when the pain becomes too much.

An automatic response kicked in. To me, a hospice is where

you go to die, and even though I'm staring down the barrel of death, I'm not ready to go there yet.

Mum swooped in on Wednesday and managed to take care of what was important – the children – so I could focus on myself. If I can continue to manage, I will not be going into a hospice.

I don't want to die.

It's as simple as that!

I DO NOT WANT TO DIE.

I don't want to leave. I've got so much more that I want to do. There's so much more I need to bear witness to.

Taking my beautiful babies to school, watching them grow, seeing them become the amazing people I know they will be.

I'm not ready to not be a part of all that.

Lexie held my hand so tightly as I walked her to her classroom this morning.

"Are you all right, sweetie?" I asked.

"Oh yes, Mummy, I'm fine. I'm squeezing you extra tight to help make you feel better."

She's such a precious soul and will do great things in this world, of that I have no doubt.

As I was eating last night's pizza (it was soooooooooo good by the way!) I texted Lawson:

> The kids are fine and in school, will you be home in time for dinner tonight?

43

Almost instantly I got a reply.

No

It was childish of me, but disappointment flooded me, not for me, but for our two beautiful babies, so I responded:

The kids will be sad that you're not home again. I can put you a dinner up for when you get in?

Again, another instant response.

No

God. I threw the last piece of pizza crust down on the plate. I don't do angry. I don't do confrontation. I don't do arguments, but God almighty!

When did it go so wrong Rob? Please tell me what I did wrong? Tell me how to make it right?

Nothing! No response! I could see the message had been read, but no response.

~

Dr Pacey has just called in. I panicked a bit because I thought

I'd forgotten an appointment!

"No, Annie, I was passing and wanted to make sure you were ok after the past couple of days?"

"Oh gosh, I'm feeling so much better. The new pain meds seem to be working really well – I've even felt hungry!"

"That's wonderful. I've spoken to Dr Prescott this morning. We are both…concerned, Annie. We understand and respect your decision not to tell your loved ones about what's going on. But how will you cope – practically? Towards the end you're going to need help. Rob will need answers, either before or soon after…"

I knew what he was trying to tell me. If I wasn't going to tell Lawson I was dying, then I needed to be able to tell him after I'd gone.

"Will you help me?" I asked him.

"Any way I can, Annie, and I know Dr Prescott will do too."

"Ok, I'll take on board what you've said."

"Here, take this, it's got all my contact numbers on, including my personal mobile – call me anytime and I will do everything I possibly can to help you, Annie. You're not alone in this." With that he left, and a trail of thoughts and realisations followed in his wake.

~

Dinner this evening with the kids was great. As Lawson didn't want to eat with us, I decided to treat us and we had a takeaway

45

and ate in the living room with their favourite films. It was bloody fab.

They truly are amazing children, and I feel incredibly proud to be their momma.

Putting them to bed was no hassle; they were both sparked out before I'd even turned the lights out! I will admit that I sat slumped against the landing wall silently sobbing. Beau crept up the stairs, even though she knows she's not allowed up here. She pushed her snout into my hands and allowed me to hold her tight as the waves of sadness washed over me. I don't want to leave them.

I'm their momma. I'm the one who's meant to tuck them into bed each and every night.

I'm supposed to tell them I love them more than the moon.

I'm supposed to be the one that washes the mud from between their toes.

I'm the one that's supposed to smother them in kisses and cuddles each day.

Is it being taken away from me?

Do I feel cheated?

I don't know, but I felt total helplessness at that moment, holding Beau as I struggled to regain control.

As my breathing calmed, I knew what I needed to do. I had to take back control.

This IS happening to me; I can't control that, but I CAN control how I choose to respond to it.

I'm going to put together some sort of package for Lawson to have once it's over. I'll give it to Dr Pacey to give to him.

I'm also going to ask for help. Something I struggle with. I'm going to see Mum and Dad tomorrow; I'm going to need them.

I'm going to regain control.

It's 9.30pm now and Lawson still isn't home.

Saturday 02 April

Sunday 03 April

This weekend I've felt good, and I've enjoyed every second of it with my babies. Squeezing out every drop of happiness we could. We laughed, played, and picnicked. Beau walking in the Meadow, rolled on the grass, went fairy hunting, bug hunting, visiting Janey was great on Sunday. She's such a wonderful grandmother.

Lawson was moody for most of the weekend, almost baying for a fight.

"Is anything wrong, love?" I asked after he'd slammed the kitchen cupboard closed.

"Why the fuck should there be anything wrong?" He stormed out, grabbed Beau's lead and slammed the front door.

Saturday we visited my folks and Andy was there, so a rather intense water fight broke out in the back garden – I'm still not sure who actually won, Andy or the kids. Either way they all look like they'd been drowned when they came back in the house, exhausted and utterly thrilled.

While they frolicked over Dad's prized roses, I told Mum and Dad about Dr Pacey's visit, and my plan to allow Lawson to know everything, once the time was right. I also vocalised for the first time my desire to be able to regain control.

"Darling, whatever you need, just ask," Dad said as he encased my hands in his. "How soon do you need the money?"

"Honestly? I've no idea! I don't even know if what I want to do is possible. I had a look last night and I found a local funeral director called Thompson and Morgan. I was going to ring them on Monday and see if I can go and see them," I said. Looking at my parent's faces, I could see they were crumbling.

"Phone now, darling. Places like that don't close! I'll go and make us some tea and then we can draw up a battle plan. How does that sound?" Mum has always been the practical one – 'A good list always goes a long way', that's what she's always said.

I phoned the funeral director there and then and spoke to a lovely man called Richard. He said it's very common these days to plan and pay for your funeral before the event. A lot of folks like knowing that what's going to happen isn't someone else's idea of a 'good funeral'! I've got an appointment with him this morning at 9.30am after I've dropped the kids off at school.

I must confess I'm feeling calm. I thought I'd be nervous. After all, I'm going to talk about my bloody funeral. But I'm not. Taking back control is absolutely the right thing to do.

~

I'll get to the funeral director visit in a second. First I need to share something gut-wrenching that happened after I'd picked the kids up. We were driving back home when Lex said, "Mommy, why does Daddy never seem happy anymore?"

My observant little girl never misses much.

"Oh, sweetie, Daddy is happy. He's just very busy at work now, and that takes a lot of his time. I don't think he means to be unhappy when he's with us."

It's the best I could come up with on the spot. It was kind of a half-truth, but not the whole truth.

I've just put them to bed and covered them in kisses, and I have decided this cannot continue. So, I'm going to wait up until Lawson gets home and have it out once and for all.

Now for my appointment with Richard at the funeral director's.

He is such a wonderful man, totally suited to his job! Very kind, compassionate, softly spoken and understanding.

Richard walked me through the whole process from the start (or end). He explained in detail what would happen to my body once I've gone, and when his firm will become involved. We walked together out of his office, across the car park and into a separate building.

It was a beautiful building with arched stained-glass windows and a single wooden arched door.

"This is the chapel of rest, Annie. This is where your family will be able to come and visit you. A space where they can come together and spend as much time with you as they need to. Come on in." He held the door open for me.

We walked into a beautifully tastefully decorated room with three further wooden doors leading off.

"Each of these three rooms holds an individual private chapel of rest." Richard gestured to the doors. "They are all vacant now if you'd like to look inside at each one? They are all decorated slightly differently."

"Thank you, Richard. Yes, I'd like to see them."

We moved into the first room. It was brightly decorated with heavy drapes across the large windows. Spotlights cast just enough shadows, without being too bright. In the corner of the room was a collection of soft chairs with a candle stand next to them.

In the middle of the room stands a catafalque – which Richard told me is what the coffin will stand up on. The coffin will be brought from the main refrigeration unit into the chapel prior to any visit.

We moved on to the middle room; that had a darker feel, thanks to the smaller windows. It was also a smaller space.

"Some people like small space. It helps them feel closer to their loved ones," Richard explained, as he showed me around.

Finally, we entered the door on the right-hand side. It was flooded with sunlight streaming through the stained-glass windows, creating dancing rainbows across the wooden floor. Beautiful classical music was playing in the background.

Two soft chairs sat close to one of the arched windows, and the candle stand stood in front of the other.

Again, a catafalque stood in the middle of the room.

"As with the other two rooms, this will remain exclusively for you and your family's use whilst you are in our care. The coffin in placed in the centre of the room, with the lid lent up against this wall, so your family can see the name plate."

"What's that door?" I asked as I noticed another door on the other side of the room.

"That's the door through to our backroom area. That's where we prepare our clients prior to their ceremonies and visitations." He's so professional.

Basically a nice way of saying that's where all the work goes on! Definitely not part of the standard tour!!!

"I like this room a lot. It feels airy – light and welcoming," I said as I walked over to the windows and touched the glass. "I think I'd like Rob to see me in here." I turned to face Richard.

"Of course, Annie. If you're happy, we'll head back to my office to talk through everything else." He guided me out of the chapel of rest. "Is there anything specific you've been thinking you'd like, Annie?" he asked as he locked the chapel door.

"Yes," I said as I followed him back into the main building. "I'd like a pale-coloured coffin, nothing dark."

"We have a few brochures – let's have a look. We have some very traditional-looking options or perhaps you'd like something a little more natural – how about a water hyacinth construction?" He reached behind his desk and opened a brochure showing me the coffin.

It was perfect, so simple, so serene, so 'me', with rope handles and simple cotton and linen lining.

"That's exactly what I want." I smiled at Richard as he watched me.

"Ok, great." He made a note on his pad.

"I don't want to be embalmed, Richard. I don't want those chemicals pumped into me."

"That's ok, Annie. It is advisable, especially if you would like your family to see you. But I completely understand your reasoning." Again, he made another note.

"Have you thought about the type of service you'd like?"

"Nothing too fancy. We aren't a religious family." I smiled, hoping not to offend him.

"Ok, if you're not wanting a religious service, I would recommend the crematorium. It has outstanding far-reaching views across the open countryside. That is, if you would like to have a service?"

"The crematorium is fine. I have attended a few funerals there and it is beautiful."

He paused as he wrote again. "Would you prefer a burial or cremation? Either option is available to you."

"Cremation. Then I'd like the ashes to be given to Rob to be scattered at Watermouth in North Devon."

"These are a few of the popular urns we've got, or we can order a particular type if you'd prefer."

"This one is lovely." I indicated a silver-toned roundish pot.

He scribbled away again. "We need to prepare an order

of service. Here are a few examples." He moved four examples across his desk.

All of them were lovely – really, they were. Although the fourth one stood out as it was simple, unfussy, and just perfect.

"This one, I think," I said, sliding it back towards him.

"Ok, we'll need a photograph of you for the front page. Also, do you have any requests for readings or a eulogy?"

"A eulogy from my brother Andy – Andrew Stephens. I'd like my favourite piece of poetry, 'Desiderata', read by our dear friend Zak Matthews and a poem read at my grandmother's funeral called 'The Dash' to be read by my dad, Malcolm Stephens. Although Rob or any of them may say different. I don't want any of them to feel that they have to do any of it," I clarified.

"That's great, Annie," he said as he wrote it all down. "What I'll do is pull all this information together for your personalised plan. Any music?"

"'Over the Rainbow' when we arrive, please. And then I'd really like to do something a bit unusual," I said, nervously.

"Oh, go on?" Richard smiled; he really had a calming nature.

"I'd like 'Walking on Sunshine' to be played towards the end."

"What a lovely song." He grinned.

"But I'd like to encourage those who attend to sing along. I don't want the ceremony to be a sad affair; I want it to be a celebration of the fact that I lived, and I have had a happy life."

"Annie, that's a lovely idea. I'll make sure it happens," he said reassuringly. "Anything else?"

"I don't want the children to see me once I'm here with you. I think I'd like Rob to decide if he wants to have your cars to go to the ceremony."

"Of course. I can talk through the options with Rob," he reassured me.

"Richard, there's something I need you to know. Rob doesn't know that I'm poorly. He doesn't know that I'm... leaving." I don't know why I felt ashamed to say it. "It's all going to come as a shock to him. He's going to need..."

"Help?" He finished what I couldn't.

"Yes."

"Of course, Annie. I understand. We will do everything we can to help Rob cope and make the decisions that are right for all of you."

"Thank you, Richard."

"We will need to put a password on the account to give Rob access to all the information. What word would you like?" he asked.

"Watermouth," I confirmed.

"Have you considered a gathering after the ceremony?" He looked up at me from his forms.

"I have a favourite place called The Boat Shack. It's a beautiful setting overlooking a lake – just stunning. I haven't spoken to Karen, the owner, yet but I will, and I'll organise everything and make sure it's all paid for. Is it ok to let you know when I've spoken to her and it's all booked?"

"Yes, of course." He wrote all this information on his pad. "I'll liaise with her regarding dates and times when needed. We will also need to know if you'd like to be dressed in your own clothes or we have a shroud if that's more convenient?"

"Oh! I'll find some of my own clothes, if that's ok? Can I bring them in to you?"

"Yes, whenever you're ready. What about flowers?"

"I think our children might like to be involved in that. Perhaps they could decide?"

"I'll include some ideas in the brochure I'll give to Rob when the time comes," Richard said, closing his folder, indicating he'd asked everything he needed to.

"Thank you for all your help today, Richard." I stood up to leave. "I feel more settled knowing that everything is sorted."

"It's been wonderful to meet you, Annie." He shook my hand. "I wish we'd met under happier circumstances," he said sadly.

"Thank you, Richard."

As I opened the office door, he added: "Annie, I promise personally that we'll look after you."

I smiled at him and then had to leave as the tears were flowing.

I sat in the car staring back at the funeral director's building through bleary eyes. I looked out of the driver side window at the chapel of rest.

I smiled.

I smiled as the tears fell onto my lap.

I'm happy to come here.

I like this place. It's...peaceful.

It's going to be the best of a bad situation. No matter how much I wish, it simply cannot be changed, and I'll be happy for those I love and who love me to come and be with me one last time in this place.

Tuesday 05 April

He rocked up at 10.36pm last night! He shut the living room door and turned on the TV. Didn't even come upstairs to kiss the kids!

Rude!

So, I went downstairs, turned off the TV, much to his disgust, and spoke my truth quietly and clearly. I have never shouted at him and I never will.

I said: "Something has shifted in our marriage. I am deeply upset, and you are clearly unhappy – even Lex sees it. She asked me on the way home why you're always unhappy. So, what do we need to do to make this right again? I love you and I will always. All I want to do is make you and our children happy."

To say that what happened next deeply shocked me would be an understatement.

He just sat there staring at the fireplace, not at me, almost like he was deciding his next move.

He banged his fist down on the arm of the sofa, stood up and looked me square in the face.

"I'm going to Berlin next week for work. I'll be gone Monday to Friday."

Then he walked out of the room and upstairs.

I was left standing alone in the living room. I could feel myself shaking with shock. The only thing I could hear was the boiler firing up as he turned the shower on.

I stayed downstairs and sat with Beau, then curled up on the sofa all night, trying to digest what had happened.

Was it the end?

Was I wrong?

Was everything ok?

Why is it all falling apart?

Getting the kids up, dressed and breakfasted will hopefully allow me a moment's respite from the endless questions.

At Mum and Dad's on Saturday, I arranged to visit Andy today to see the new flat he's just moved into. And I need to tell him – I must be the one to tell him.

~

The flat was absolutely gorgeous, and perfect for him – it even had a garage for his motorbike tinkering stuff he so loves to do.

I love my big brother; he is a fantastic uncle and such a source of strength for me. Just those two years between us and he's always been my best friend. His divorce last year has left many scars, but he's doing so well now.

Telling him about Hector wouldn't be so bad. I think I had

built it up in my head, but when I went to say it, it would be ok. After all, it's just a word, isn't it?

We were sitting surrounded by boxes, drinking tea from the teapot that Mum had given him as a housewarming present.

"Andy, I need to tell you something." I took a deep breath and reached across the table and took his hand, just like I did when we were little. I said "Squidge" (my nickname for him) and took another deep breath. "Squidge, I'm ill. Really ill."

He pulled away from me slightly, looking at my face.

"Squidge, it's cancer." He withdrew his hand and put it across his mouth, clearly trying to stifle a cry.

"You'll be ok though, Mouse," he said, using his nickname for me. "There are loads of different treatments and options available these days," he added with positivity.

I simply shook my head as tears fell.

"NO!" escaped from my brother's very core. He stood up and rounded the table, grabbing me and pulling me up and into an all-consuming hug.

"It's weeks, Squidge. Just weeks." The snot was flowing – gross!

"It's ok, baby girl, it's ok. Squidge has got you," he kept repeating while stroking my hair.

What was bad was watching as I destroyed my brother's world. Watching as he crumpled in pain. That is what is truly hard.

I just held him as he sobbed, apologised, sobbed some more

and then apologised all over again. All I could do was keep repeating "I love you".

I explained about my decision not to tell Lawson or the kids, and he vocalised exactly what I knew to be true in my very soul.

"Let your last days with them be your best days with them."

Andy has always viewed the world in a similar way to me. In the past, some people have even said we are more like twins, and it's true. He gets me and I him.

As I was leaving, he held me so tight and told me: "Please know you are so loved, Mouse."

It's weird because I know I'm loved, I really do! With that knowledge comes reassurance and so much responsibility. The people who love me, rely on me, depend on me, look to me, and need me.

In an unknown number of days, all those people whom I love in return are going to be irreparably broken by my leaving – that carries a heavy weight.

~

As I was driving to school Andy texted and said he was on his way to collect the kids as he'd like to take them out for tea! So, I turned the car around and headed home.

Just as I pulled up on the drive my phone rang. A lady called Carole introduced herself and said she was calling from Macmillan and wanted to let me know about all the support that is available to me and the family if I need it. I was half-listening as I was more focused on Lawson's car being on the drive – he was never home at this time of day!

People are so kind when they are dealing with death – perhaps it's a prerequisite for getting a job in that profession?

I thanked her and asked her if she could send everything over by email and I would look.

As I got out of the car and was about to unlock the front door, the phone went again! It was like a bloody hotline!

It was Dr Prescott's secretary asking me to go in to see her next Tuesday as the results of all my latest tests will be back by then.

God, who knew dying would require so much administration, planning and organising?

Lawson's open suitcase was lying on the bed – he was packing for his trip.

"You're home early," I said as I walked into the room.

"Not for long. I've come home to change and then I'm back out again," he mumbled.

"Do you want me to finish packing for you?" I offered, as I opened his sock drawer.

"No."

That was it – he was gone from the house again, to return at an unknown time later this evening.

~

Dinner was just me, so I had my favourite – bread and butter with tomato sauce on top! So delish.

Andy and the kids came home after having a secret spy dinner at an undisclosed location that may or may not have included chips.

We also had bath-time switching – one in the bath, one in the shower, then switching! Bubbles everywhere!

Wednesday 06 April

Happy birthday, Beau! Seven years of sock-stealing! She is such a gentle soul – the kids made her wear a party hat at breakfast. She really does put up with a lot of stuff that poor dog. We don't talk about the 'pony' rides when the kids were younger. Halloween costumes! She made a great ghost!!!

I spent a lot of time thinking last night – Dr Pacey is right. I need to get my affairs in order. I've always found that saying ridiculous, but it's true. You need to get everything sorted before you run out of time.

Time is something I no longer have. I didn't even realise I possessed it until I was told it had been taken away.

That train of thought went thundering through so many different stations and locations, I felt thoroughly exhausted by the time I finally nodded off.

However, somewhere I did stop on that train-of-thought journey was our honeymoon destination at Watermouth. Just Lawson and me as we walked the rugged landscape of North Devon. We had such a wonderful time. No rushing. We didn't worry; we didn't have the stresses that come with day-to-day life.

Lawson was the happiest I'd ever seen him – until our two babies came along. He was at peace; we were both at peace. We ate wonderful food, drank probably way too much, relaxed in the bubbles of our own hot tub watching the sun setting over Cove Harbour.

It was so far away from where we both are right now.

That week was utter bliss.

Can we somehow recapture that?

As I was making the kids' breakfasts, Dr Prescott's office called and I'm now sitting in the waiting room of the endoscopic ultrasound department. I feel today isn't going to be the day I'd planned.

~

I'm so bloody sore!

That woman had me lying in all sorts of different shapes – so homemade burgers and salad for dinner! Thank goodness for a few months ago when I'd had a day of batch cooking!

Lawson came home surprisingly early and joined us as we watched kids' TV before bedtime.

For that short time it was like having my family back together again – no awkwardness, just us, the four of us.

After the kids had gone to sleep, I'd hoped Lawson would want to continue our enjoyable evening, but after taking a shower and seeing all the random bruises all over my body I'm quietly glad that he hid himself away in the study.

The divide between us is not his fault. It's circumstance and both of us are idiots – that much I do know!

He is a wonderful man. He has the best sense of humour ever. He is the only person who's been able to make me laugh even in my darkest times – a smile that can light up a room. His eyes – that's what first attracted me to him. Like the deepest ocean – you could get lost in them. He was and is one of the most handsome men I've ever seen. My heart still skips a beat when I watch him sometimes, just like it did nearly fifteen years ago when I first met him.

God, I remember the first time I saw him. I'll never forget that! Literally, my stomach dropped away when he walked into the café. I'd never ever seen anyone so handsome. Whenever he was in my presence, I seemed to turn into a giddy schoolgirl, incapable of pouring boiling water into a cup.

I lived for the days when I worked in the café in the hope that the handsome chap would come in.

Black coffee with one sugar and carrot cake! HA! I can still remember his order!

I tried so hard to 'play it cool' when he started to talk to me and then when he started visiting the café every time I was working.

I was a bag of nerves when I saw him walking towards me as I sat outside at the back of the café on my break, sketchbook on my lap.

"Can I join you?" he asked as he sat down.

GOD ALMIGHTY! He was cool personified.

"Sure," I managed to utter.

"What are you drawing?" He leant closer to me.

I struggled to focus as I smelled his aftershave; he smelled so – clean?

Play it cool, Stephens, play it cool, was all I could say to myself.

"Just those children over there playing by the water's edge." I pointed with my pencil.

"Cool! You're good." His smile dazzled me. "I'm Rob, by the way, Rob Lawson."

"Nice to meet you, Lawson. I'm Annie Stephens." I smiled back, shyly.

"Oh, I know you're Annie," he replied. I was rocked to my core – he knows my name! How does he know who I am? "It says so on your name badge!" He sniggered.

He made my heart sing.

He still makes my heart sing.

I loved him within thirty seconds of clapping my eyes on him, and I still love him now.

Today started grim – weather-wise, health-wise, attitude-wise and generally-giving-a-toss-wise.

It's not often that I get 'pissed off' but today is one of those days. If I didn't know better I'd say I was suffering from PMT but I haven't had a period in over eighteen months.

Everything is irritating me, noises, smells, even my clothes – everything.

Lawson unfortunately caught the full force of my irritation.

The morning school dash was exactly that – a dash! We only just made it to the school gates with seconds to spare. I was so thankful to get back into the quiet of the house, just me and Beau.

For some reason my mobile didn't charge last night, so the battery was dead. I realised just as I got home, and plugged it in on the kitchen counter and began the daily round of kitchen reconstruction after the kids eat breakfast. How they manage to get the toast under the radiator is beyond me!

My phone rang almost instantly. I didn't even get to say hello...

"Where the hell have you been?" Lawson spat at me.

"Dropping the kids off. I've just got back."

"I've been trying to ring you – the school have rung me! I had to come out of a meeting to answer it!!!" Venom laced his every word.

"Oh my God! What's wrong? Are they ok? My phone didn't charge last night. I've just plugged it in."

"For God sake, Annie! Lexie has forgotten her lunch box!" he spat at me.

I turned on the spot and sitting there staring back at me was Lexie's pink unicorn lunch box, exactly where it was when I asked her to pick it up forty minutes earlier.

"I'm working. I can't come away from meetings for such nonsense!"

Something snapped. As I sit now and reflect I know it wasn't at all anything to do with Lawson. It wasn't his fault. I didn't mean to do it. It was definitely wrong place, wrong time.

In my defence I didn't shout at him, but I also didn't stop for breath!

"Nonsense? No, it's not nonsense that our daughter has nothing to eat! It's not nonsense that my phone didn't charge! It's not nonsense that you're accusing me of somehow doing any of this to in some way sabotage your day! Do you know what is nonsense? Do you know what is a joke? Our marriage. That's what's a fucking joke!" I ended the call, picked up the lunch box and left the mobile on the counter top.

I've calmed down now – clearly, I needed something to eat! So, a nice round of jam on toast and I'm back to something resembling a proper human.

I'm sitting in the conservatory with Beau at my feet. I've left my mobile unattended all morning. It has rung on and off and beeped with multiple messages.

I know I need to hoist up those big-girl pants again and apologise to Lawson, but I'm finding it difficult.

I don't think it's the apology I'm struggling with. It's simply admitting that I've no idea how he's going to cope when I'm not here. How will he juggle work and school and all the after-school clubs that will come in the near future?

I'm going to ask Mum to pick up the kids tomorrow. I need to begin preparations, and that involves a very long drive! I'm going back down to Watermouth to see the sea one more time.

~

The children were golden this evening, both wanting hugs without even being asked! I treasure these moments. Now safely tucked up in bed, all I can hear is their gentle snores – it's so soothing.

It's 8.45pm and Lawson still isn't home. I did the right thing earlier and grabbed my phone and texted an apology to him for how I behaved earlier. Am I surprised that none of the messages I'd received throughout the day were from him? Nope!

The messages were from Mum and Andy asking if I was ok. Andy asked if he can do anything around the house. Cutting the grass? Cleaning the windows? Serenading me through the front door? Mum wanted to know if we needed anything from the shop as she and Dad are off out to town tomorrow.

Agghhhh coffee, a warm blanket and my sunnies on.

I'm here at Watermouth. The journey down wasn't too bad. How long is the M5 though? It is relatively quiet down here now, but the harbour is always buzzing with folks coming and going, tinkering with their beloved boats – it is, after all, a working harbour. Give it a few weeks and the tourists will arrive in their droves, folks memory-making. They will fill the picnic tables; kids will paddle in the stream as the water makes its way out to sea. They'll build sandcastles when the tide is out and have the most wonderful time.

The sun is glistening off the water as the tide comes into the sheltered harbour.

I've brought a bundle of greetings cards with me, and I intend to spend the morning ensuring Lexie and Louis will have a little something from me for the foreseeable future and every birthday and Christmas.

Lawson came home about 9.30pm last night. I was dozing but heard him go into the en suite and turn the shower on. He didn't say a word to me.

I'd had enough. I only have a certain amount of energy and right now it's being spread very thinly – I need to sort out my marriage before it's too late.

So, I got out of bed and went into the en suite, opened the shower cubicle door, and climbed in, PJs and all, next to him.

"What the hell, Ann?" he shouted, his face covered in bubbles.

Water was streaming down my face, my pyjamas sticking to my shrinking body.

"I need to say I'm sorry, Lawson. I need to say it to your face. I shouldn't have overreacted earlier, and I shouldn't have taken it out on you."

My husband stared down at me, open-mouthed.

"This isn't the time, Ann!" He turned his back to me and began washing his body again.

I grabbed his elbow and turned him back around, my tears merging with the falling water. "When is the time, Rob? Because from where I'm standing it seems like you're doing everything you can to avoid that time." My voice was shaking.

I looked my husband square in the eyes, begging him, willing him to read my very soul. I watched as he clenched and unclenched his jaw.

He continued to stare at me, the shower raining down on both of us.

"Pleas…" was all I managed to say before he pushed me up

against the glass of the shower wall and kissed me. Kissed me with such force that it took my breath away. Needless to say, it became a very enjoyable shower!

Waking up this morning to find arms around me rather than a cold bed has lifted my spirits, although last night's activities have left me feeling internally and externally sore and tender.

As I sit now, staring out across the harbour, I'm feeling quietly hopeful that Lawson and I are beginning to see each other again. I love him and that's what makes Hector even harder to accept and swallow.

I know writing these cards is going to be hard, but also easy at the same time. Telling my children how truly treasured they are isn't going to be difficult. I've never had trouble telling my children how much they mean to me, how much joy they have each brought into my life. How their arrival fulfilled a lifelong dream within me to be a mother.

Thankfully, the lovely little boat café was open. The nice owner was telling me that they've decided to open Friday, Saturday, and Sunday and in a couple of weeks they'll move to seven days a week. Jennifer and Jeff have owned The Teacup since 'the dawn of time' apparently! Although they are considering selling up later this year as they both feel ready to retire. While sitting on the bench chatting to Jennifer as she took a break, I had a blast of inspiration and asked Jen if I wrote a letter and gave her some money would she keep hold of it?

I wrote a letter to you, Lawson – though you probably know that by now:

See, sitting there in the sunshine, shielded from the world by the high banks of the coastline, I knew – I knew that this is where you are meant to be. You're meant to come to Watermouth. You must raise our children in a place where they can run free on the beach and splash in the waves whenever they want. Beau – oh, my goodness – Beau will adore coastal walks and splashing in the surf – chasing the crests of the waves.

~

I'm absolutely exhausted! Today has made me realise that my energy levels aren't what they once were. Driving to Devon and back in a day is something that I wouldn't have thought twice about a few years ago.

Mum ordered a Chinese takeaway for dinner; it was wonderful to see the kids having a heated debate over who had the biggest prawn cracker.

Today has been very productive. I feel better for knowing that I'm preparing.

Lawson got home just as the kids were going to sleep and his mood was foul!

When I asked him what was wrong, he muttered something about work and slammed the study door. One step forward, two steps back.

I'm not sure what I'm meant to do. Maybe I should go into

the study now and tell him exactly what's going on, tell him about Hector?

Make him realise that this is nonsense, the gap between us.

Make him realise that our time together is running out.

That the sands of time are slipping away from me?

All that matters is that we love each other.

Unless... Unless he doesn't love me anymore?

Maybe our life isn't enough for him anymore?

God, I'd never even considered the possibility that he may not love me anymore – holy fuck!

Saturday 09 April

Very little sleep thanks to last night's revelation – am I self-destructing? Am I trapping him? Do I want my marriage to fall apart? Am I having a pity party? Am I entitled to one?

I think overall that I am a positive person, not a lot fazes me. But, Jesus, I feel like my foundations are crumbling underneath me.

I'm scared...

I'm terrified...

I'm petrified of leaving...

I'm petrified of losing my husband...

But I'm not afraid of actually dying!

While everyone slept last night, I went down to the study and spent some time looking for a local organisation that can help with bereavement. I found an amazing organisation called The Lavender Trust, which will support children through their grief. It's comforting to know that there are people out there who could help them once I've gone. Not that I feel Lawson won't be able to help the children, but he's going to need all the help he can get.

I hope that when the time is right, Lawson will find that

I've bookmarked them on the internet browser.

He's currently in the shower. I really hope his mood has improved today, and we can have a family day. His mobile has just pinged with a message arriving; it's just sitting on the side charging…

Should I look?

I trust him…

Don't I…?

But he wasn't talking to Zak…?

I could look…?

I'm going to look…

NO…!

Yeah just a peek…

NO!!!! STOP IT!!!!!!!!!

Looking forward to Monday. Will be much easier when we're there

Sent from Ben.

I don't remember Lawson mentioning a Ben, but I'm glad he's got a supportive colleague…

Another bling…

XXX

What THE FUCK.

~

The kids are staying with Janey tonight.

I did not go home after dropping them off.

I'm currently sitting in the Hanbury Ring, our local craft centre. They sell expensive coffee, amazing cake and loads of nick-nacks that no one needs but everyone will always want once they see them.

Keeping me company is a double choc-chip cake and a cafetière of the finest Columbian coffee.

The big-girl pants were pulled back on earlier when I asked Lawson who Ben was.

His face went ashen white, and he fumbled for his words.

I know deep down in my heart that Ben isn't a Ben – it's probably code.

I've lost him.

That hurts more than Hector. I've lost my husband to someone else.

The tears are falling silently. I'm trying not to draw attention to myself. I've put my sunnies on, hoping people will think I've got hayfever or I'm some sort of superstar!

I'm acutely aware that when I go to the clinic on Tuesday, Dr Prescott is going to comment on my weight. I know I've lost a bit. My appetite is hit and miss – some days I feel I could eat a horse, the next, nothing.

But for now, I'm enjoying watching the ducks gliding across the pond and savouring the flavour of the coffee.

~

I've just finished a video call with the kids. Janey has made an indoor camp on the floor with lots of cushions and duvets. Apparently, they're all going to sleep there.

"Nan, let me try some of her leftover curries – it was scrummy. Can you make me some, please?" said a very sleepy-looking Lexie.

"Of course! You'll have to ask Nan for the recipe?" I smiled at her. She really is so beautiful.

"NANNNNNNNNNN, Mummy needs you to tell her how to make more of that curry for my belly!"

~

Tonight, I've just hidden away, hidden away from food, life, husbands, Hector, life, my fate.

I feel like a wall is about to break and whatever's behind it is going to consume me. I've no way to stop it.

My world is crumbling around me.

Am I losing the fight?

NO

I'm not losing the fight!!!!

Today, while the kids are still with Janey, Mum is coming over and we're going shopping for presents. We are going to store them at Mum and Dad's house until they are all wrapped.

It's a beautiful start to the day. I'm sitting in the conservatory enjoying the warm sunshine as Beau dashes in and out of the garden, creating muddy paw prints all over the clean floor – but I'm not even bothered. Floors can always be cleaned; fun should never be stopped.

Lawson came down just now and muttered about leaving at 6pm tonight and staying in a hotel close to the airport to catch the 4.30am plane tomorrow.

I couldn't even respond. Fear paralysed me. I just couldn't find the words to respond.

Perhaps these few days apart will give us both space and time to think?

~

Mum and I are home!!!!!

The kids are home!!!!!

Normal service has resumed as soon as they barged through the door.

~

I am exhausted again! We've bought what feels like most of the toy store, vouchers, jewellery, watches and finally holiday vouchers for both kids' birthdays and Christmases until they are twenty-one.

I gave the stack of cards I wrote in Devon to Mum to go with the presents, while I make room here for them to be hidden. I don't want them found before, well, before...

By the time we got the kids back from Janey's (5.35pm to be exact), Lawson's car wasn't on the drive. He'd left early. He'd left without even saying goodbye.

That was the moment when I allowed all the excess energy I'd been using up by fretting and worrying to leave my body. I gave a metaphorical sigh of relief. For a few days, I don't have to worry about Lawson catching sight of me when I get out of the shower and asking why my body looks the way it does.

I don't have to worry what mood he'll be in, or if he'll be

home in time to kiss our children goodnight.

I can focus everything on my beautiful children, preparing for when – and embrace every moment that is given to me.

I love my husband, but I officially resign from fretting just for a few days. The next days are about our mess makers. I cannot and will not play this game. Either he loves me or he doesn't. I will not force him to stay somewhere he isn't happy. I will never wish for him to be anything but happy each day of his life.

This week I am focusing on whatever future I have.

The shopping trip with Mum, although exhausting, was enjoyable. Spending time alone together, having girly chats, gossiping, and laughing. We never once spoke about what's happening or what's to come. It was just like it should be when a mum and daughter spend time together.

Monday 11 April

I slept so well last night, there is the smallest possibility I might have star-fished a bit in bed! Well, come on, everyone does it when they have the bed to themselves, don't they?

The house was so calm this morning. The kids were as good as gold. Even Beau was good – she didn't steal a single sock. We walked to school in the lovely spring sunshine.

I haven't heard from Lawson yet, but that's ok. I'm actively choosing to not allow this pettiness to bother me anymore.

I'm feeling nervous about tomorrow and what will be said. It's not like I can be given any more bad news. I just don't want them to say I've got less time than they thought. I need every second I can get.

Mum offered to come with me, while we were out yesterday. She really has been my rock over the past few weeks. I'm so lucky that Mum is amazing.

~

It's such a wonderful feeling knowing everyone has had a good day.

I loved hearing all about Lexie's day, and how excited Louis was about the new sand toys they've got in the nursery. It's unbelievable how quickly they grow.

They are both so happy and relaxed, I am happy and relaxed, which is a total contradiction to the war that is currently raging its way throughout my body.

~

The kids spoke to Lawson this evening on a video call. He was in his hotel room. They loved it, and even insisted on a tour of his room.

I know she was there. I heard her. He denied it. But I know.

Am I worried?

Am I scared?

Am I hurt?

Am I angry?

Honestly?

No.

I'm ok.

I really am ok.

I'm focusing on myself.

Sometimes you must pull back and focus on yourself. It's not that you are being selfish, or self-centred; it is simply what you must do.

I truly don't blame my husband. Life has a way of directing your journey along a path that you'd never freely walk down but walk down it you must.

Well, today didn't start as I'd planned! Lexie woke with a temperature and a cough!

I've just phoned Mum and asked if she can come over and look after Lex, while I go to the appointment, as I'm not going to send her to school.

She said to bring her over to their house and they'll look after her all day.

So, I bundled the children into the car, dropped Lou off, and went straight over to Mum and Dad's. Dad shocked me.

"Off you two go. My little girl and I will be fine without you," he said, as he ushered me and Mum out of the door.

Dad had never looked after the grandkids alone – ever. He always liked to know that Mum was nearby 'just in case'.

"Off you go, May, look after my big girl." He shooed Mum further out of the door.

My heart melted; my old dad is becoming sentimental.

We arrived with plenty of time at the hospital. So, we went into the RVS café to grab a coffee. Mum nipped into the hospital shop to get some sweets for the kids when we get back, and not any sweets for Dad!

Wish me luck…

~

I'm back home and the kids are in bed.

Dr Prescott's clinic was running on time as always. She is an incredibly efficient medical practitioner, but then I go in for my appointment and make everyone behind me wait – sorry, peeps!

Mum was happy to sit in the waiting room, but when I was called in, I suddenly realised I needed her with me.

"It's not good news, Annie," Dr Prescott said, after we had introductions and exchanged pleasantries. "Progression is fast. Growth is large and your prognosis has shifted." She struggled to look me in the eyes.

"How long?" I remained calm. I could see Mum's shoulders moving out of the corner of my eye, as silent sobs racked her body. I knew if I looked at her my resolve would collapse.

"If you're careful and don't overdo things, three weeks at the most. Annie, I'm so terribly sorry." She reached across her desk to take my hand and offer reassurance. Now she was looking at me and tears were filling her eyes.

A sob escaped Mum's mouth and I tightened my grip on her hand.

"Right, then." I composed myself. "We best get memory-making, hadn't we!" I turned and smiled at my beautiful Mum's tear-stained face.

"Come on, Mother, I do believe there is some more carrot cake with our names on it waiting for us in the café before we head back!" All she could do was nod in agreement.

I stood up and walked around the desk and embraced Dr Prescott. "Thank you for everything you've done. Will you explain to Rob when it's time?" I asked, as her face became tear-stained as well.

"Take this." She wrote on my appointment letter. "It is my personal mobile number. I will do my best to help him," she said as she folded the paper and put it back in my hands, encasing my hands in hers. "You're being taken too soon, Annie. Thank you for lighting our days."

"Let's go, Mother, before all that cake gets sold!" I helped Mum gather her belongings – she seemed in such a state. As we were about to leave the office, I turned and looked one last time at Dr Prescott. "Thank you for everything again. I really am so grateful to you. I know I won't be seeing you again, but please know how truly lucky I feel to have had you to care for me."

Another sob escaped my mum as she held her handkerchief closer to her mouth.

"Oh, Annie, of course you'll see us again – you've got your appointment next week."

Putting my arm around Mum's shoulder to console her, I simply replied with what was in my heart. "No, Doctor, I don't need to come anymore. I know what's going to happen and sitting here today has allowed me to accept that fact and make peace with it. I just need to spend whatever time I have left saying my goodbyes and enjoying every moment. So, thank you, and goodbye."

We embraced again and she whispered, "I'll help him understand."

I told Mum to find a table while I went and got the drinks. I just needed a few moments by myself, well, even if I was standing in the queue.

I stared down at the plastic-wrapped curly sandwiches and slices of cake very near their sell-by date. Just like me. The lady behind the counter disturbed my train of thought.

"What can I get you?" she said chirpily, smiling.

I tried to smile back. I tried to form the words of my order, but all I could do was stare at her smiling, innocent face.

"More time please!" I begged.

"Sorry?" She looked confused.

"Two teas, one slice of chocolate cake and one of carrot cake, please," I managed to get out.

"Please carry on up to the till and I'll get your order ready." She smiled again.

While paying for the teas and cakes, I spotted Mum in the corner. I carried the tray to the table.

"Here you go, Mum. Put some extra sugars in your tea."

"Ann. I don't know if I can do this. I don't know if I can let you go." Tears were slowly trickling down her face.

"You're not letting me go, Mum. You've let me live. I've had the most wonderful life. I've had a happy life. I've had a colourful life. Mum, I'm who I am because of your guidance." I reached across the table and grabbed her shaking hands. "Don't be sad when I'm gone. Be happy I've been here."

"I love you so much. You're my baby girl. I don't know where you get your strength from."

"You, Mummy! You! Now come on, eat up. We need to head back and see how our little girl is doing."

Mum hardly said a word as we drove back to collect Lexie. We didn't have time to stay as I needed to get back to pick up Louis. Mum said she'd explain everything to Dad and Andy – for that I was very grateful.

~

Dinner this evening was simple – cheese toasties and salad.

I was very thankful for the kids' distraction this evening. Thankfully, a few hours alone with Grampy had clearly done the trick and cheered Lexie up no end. Although Mum has been messaging me, I haven't had the strength just yet to reply.

Now both mess-monsters are fast asleep; I'm left alone with my thoughts and this journal. I'm looking around our bedroom and all I can think is:

I wonder if this is the room I'll be in when I leave?

Hi honey. How are you feeling?

Mum clearly had processed what happened today and was ready to talk.

Hi Mum. I'm...ok. The kids are asleep, I'm just lying in bed trying to get my thoughts together. Are you and Dad alright?"

We are fine, sweetheart. I've spoken to Dad and Andy, they both send their love and extra hugs from Dad. Oh my baby girl I wish I could take this all away for you, with all my heart and soul I want to sweep you up and hold you tight until everything is better.

I started to cry. No parent, no matter how old, should ever have to witness their child leaving them.

Oh my wonderful Mum. I know you would. I remember you telling me when Lexie was born how I'd want to take away all her aches and pains, and you were right. I'd give my last breath for either of them. I love them so very dearly, and that is all thanks to you and Dad, for giving me such a wonderful example of what a parent should be.

Mum, I'm ok. Really.

Darling, how can you be ok? How are you able to

be so calm? I can hardly sleep and your Dad keeps telling me I'm not eating enough!

OH Mum! Is that true? You have to eat! Dad's right, we all need you to be as well as you can be.

I know, sweetie. But my baby is hurting and there's nothing I can do to make it better.

Mum, I'm fine. Right now I'm not in pain, I'm just tired. Just know that I really am ok. I'm not afraid of dying. I'm scared of the pain that my leaving is going to cause to you all.

MY precious precious girl. You will never leave us – not completely. Your light shines far too bright to ever be extinguished, you will shine over all of us for eternity. I love you, darling girl. Try and get a good night's sleep. Talk to you in the morning.

Night Mummy – mwah xxxxx.

Wednesday 13 April

Lawson called and spoke to the kids before school this morning. I took over the call and told him that I needed to speak to him when he gets home – it's important.

In between my bouts of restless sleep last night I decided that I have to tell him. I have to be the one that tells him I'm leaving. I'm being selfish by not telling him. I cannot continue to carry this weight by myself. He responded and said that he needs to talk to me too.

Dr Pacey visited this morning, asking me lots of questions about pain management, mobility, fluid and food intake. Once he'd finished I asked him if he'd still be willing to help me, once I'd gone.

I'm going to put together a pack of information for Lawson to have once I've gone. I'm not naive enough to think I'll be here long enough to fully explain exactly what's happening to me; he's going to want answers that I'm not going to be able to give to him.

"Let me have the package whenever you're ready, Annie. I'll make sure he gets it."

I handed Dr Pacey the big brown envelope I'd filled with all the information I could find; I included hospital appointment letters, test results, procedure leaflets and of course the letter with Dr Prescott's mobile number on. I've written on the page as well, telling Lawson to ring and ask for Tanya.

"I may need to add some more things as well, plus I'd like this book," I picked up this book and showed my wonderful GP, "to be included in the pack as well. I will always keep it in the top drawer next to my bed. If you're not able to add it into the envelope, can you direct Rob to it?"

"Of course, Annie – anything."

Outwardly I look a bit off colour and maybe a bit thinner, but nothing alarming. However, inwardly I'm being eaten alive.

~

Mum texted not long after lunch and said she'd collect the kids from school today, and insisted on coming back to our house and cooking dinner with them. Envisage culinary chaos descending.

I can't wait.

~

Lexie woke up feeling fine this morning. Kids are so resilient, aren't they? So she went into school. Watching her interactions with my mum was like looking through a time machine – just like my relationship with her all those years ago. She really was an amazing lady, and I'm so proud that she shaped me into the mother I've become and will shape Lexie if she decides to have children.

Sausage and mash was consumed with much gusto, followed by Nanny's apple crumble. Two very happy children slipped off easily into the land of nod.

Mum stayed for a quick cuppa before heading home.

"I'm sorry about yesterday, Ann. I feel a little embarrassed," she said shyly.

"What?" I spat my tea out, chuckling at my mother.

"Oi! Stop laughing at your old mum! I just want to say that I've had a long hard talk to myself, and so has your dad, and I'm now ready to do everything and anything you need me to do."

"Oh, Mum, what are you like!" I chuckled.

"Ann, is there anything we need to know, you know? About your wishes? Before you go? So we can help Rob when the time is right." She fumbled over her words.

"Oh." She took me a little by surprise. "Well, I visited the funeral director's last week. Everything there is sorted. I spoke to Dad, and he's sorted out the money for it," I said tentatively, hoping she knew.

"Yes, I know, sweetie. He went there yesterday and paid. He said it was a beautiful place. He met a man called Richard. Apparently, he was really nice."

"Oh, Mum, he really is! He's made the whole process so much easier. He's guided me and helped me make tough decisions. Everything is sorted, really. He even has some of my

clothes ready to dress me. My final wishes are with him as well."
I tried to reassure her. "Mum, everything is sorted. The only
thing that I really need help with is Rob and the kids."

She leant across and rubbed my knee. "My darling, you do
NOT need to worry about your babies and Rob. Janey, Dad,
Andy, and I will pick them up and hold them tight until they
tell us to let them go. We will love them hard until they don't
need us to anymore."

"I love you, Mum."

~

I have soaked my aching body in a long, hot bubble bath,
and I feel so much better now.

Tomorrow I plan to give my final decisions to Richard
Morgan at the funeral director's. Time to face up to the fact that
I don't have any more time.

Thursday 14 April

Dr Pacey called as I was coming home from the school run. He'd like to conduct daily home visits now I've made the decision not to return to Dr Prescott's clinic. He didn't really give me a choice but to agree.

Lawson is home tomorrow. I haven't heard from him other than when he's phoned to speak to the children. It's been bleak, but surprisingly painless.

Andy called round with the biggest bunch of flowers I've ever seen and an even bigger hug. He promised me he'd be here for Rob and the kids in whatever way they need him to be.

"Well, how rude! Bringing me something that will outlive me!"

My first joke about dying.

I'd made a joke about my death!

Andy didn't know how to respond or what to say, so I started giggling, which turned into sobbing, which opened the floodgates I'd been holding back so very tightly, released in a big mess all over my wonderful brother as I struggled to find the words to say goodbye.

~

On the way home from school, while navigating the torrential rain, the kids asked for a picnic tea!

"Picnic tea sounds amazing; I don't think we'll be able to eat in the garden," I said, as I looked at them both sitting in the back of the car.

"No, Mummy, we want a rainy picnic!" Louis responded and returned to looking out of the window.

Fumbling around my brain, trying to search for the appropriate response, I simply couldn't fathom what a 'rainy picnic' was or is! "Um, ok, champ, you're going to have to help your old mum out here – what is a 'rainy picnic'?"

"Oh, come on, Mum," Lex intervened. "It's a picnic in the conservatory so we can sit and watch and listen to the rain but still be dry!"

"Oh, yeah, silly me!" Doh!

While they filled their faces with ham sandwiches and nibbles, they both told me about their day at school. We are so lucky to have such an inspiring school.

~

Our last night without Lawson and both kids are super excited when I reminded them that Daddy would be home tomorrow. I, however, feel apprehensive, but ready. I need to tell him.

Friday 15 April

God, I've hardly had any time to even sit down and write today.

Just as I was walking Lex into school, she announced that it is Caitie's, her best friend's, birthday today.

So, there was a mad dash home to pick up the handbag.

A mad dash to The Craft Centre to purchase a 'mahussive' bucket of craft materials, then on to the garden centre to buy the most expensive wrapping paper in the world, but needs must!

Thankfully, once all the purchases were safely in the car, I decided I needed to slow down and ventured over the road to my favourite place – The Boat Shack.

After picking up a fluffy blanket from the big hamper by the door, I went inside the café and ordered a hot chocolate and ventured out onto the veranda that overlooked the lake.

For me, life slows down whenever I go to the lake. All the madness, stresses, worries and general madness of life seem to get left at the gate.

It's such a peaceful place, such a wonderful place.

As I sat there, nose-deep in squirty cream, I knew I'd made the right decision to tell Richard this is where I want everyone to come together once I've gone – after my funeral.

Thankfully, the owner, Karen, was understanding.

"Could I chat with you, Karen, about organising a wake here?" I asked as I paid my bill.

"I'm so sorry for your loss. Let me grab the function menu and we'll go back to your table and have a chat," she said as I walked back to my table.

"Tell me what sort of thing you are looking for, Annie," Karen said, as she sat down with a notebook on her lap and put a laminated menu on the table in front of me.

I started to straighten the menu level to the edge of the table, just to give my hands something to do! "Well…" I coughed to clear my throat. "I'm…umm." Coughed again. "I, well, you see…" I couldn't even look her in the face. "I'm dying, Karen. It's my wake." I looked up to see the shock cross her face.

The smile disappeared and sadness replaced it. Pity – that is what I'm trying to avoid by not telling Lawson. I don't want pity. I don't want anyone to feel sorry for me.

She managed to find some words. "Oh, Annie. I'm so terribly sorry. That's just…awful."

"It's ok, Karen, honestly. I'm starting to make peace with it. I just want to make sure everything I can organise is sorted. It means it's less for Rob, my husband, to worry about when the time comes. I'd rather he focuses on our two children."

"Of course. Of course. Oh, Annie. I am so sorry. I've enjoyed our little chats over the years – you're one of my most regular customers." She beamed a smile that seemed to come from her very soul.

"I love it here." I looked out over the water. "That's why I'd like everyone to gather here once the service is over – it's somewhere where I found peace. I've already organised my funeral and I've given the funeral director your details as I'd really like to have the wake here. So, when the time comes, he'll get in touch with dates and times. I hope I haven't been too presumptuous?"

"No, Annie, not at all. We'll do our very best to honour you and ensure that your loved ones have the opportunity to experience a slice of what you feel when you're here," she reassured me. "Let's have a look at the menu and decide what you think is best."

The Boat Shack

Function Menu

All prices are inclusive of cutlery and napkins

Menu 1

Traditional Warm Platter

Selection of sandwiches – cheese / ham / chicken / salad

Warm platter – sausage rolls / cocktail sausages / chicken nuggets

Crisp bowls – salted / cheese and onion / vegetable crisps

Cake platter – individual Victoria sponge / chocolate eclairs / chocolate brownies

Fruit platter – grapes / oranges / strawberries / raspberries

Menu 2

Traditional Cold Platter

Selection of sandwiches – cheese / ham / chicken / salad

Selection of cheese with crackers

Salad platter – celery / cherry tomatoes / cucumber / peppers / radish / lettuce

Crisp bowls – salted / cheese and onion / vegetable crisps

Cake platter – grapes / oranges / strawberries / raspberries

Menu 3

Indian Platters – Traditional Platter plus:

Onion bhajis

Saag aloo pakora

Vegetable pakora

Chicken pakora

Vegetable samosa

Tandoori chicken pieces

Mini poppadom

Mini naan breads

Spicy tomato and onion dip

Mint and yogurt dip

Selection of hot and cold refreshments available

Teas / coffee / hot chocolate / bottled water / fruit juices / milkshakes

All menus can be adapted to your size of party. Exclusive use of The Boat Shack is available as an option.

Please talk to Karen for more information, advice and to book.

~

I settled on menu one with the option of allowing Lawson to add anything else.

Karen charged me £250.00 for a maximum of 100 people. If there are any more than that, The Boat Shack will provide for them for free.

Driving home I felt – satisfied. Taking control of all I can is exactly what anyone in a similar situation should do. Dying doesn't mean you've lost everything. Ensure that the end of your life is a celebration of your life, in a way that is appropriate to your life.

I've no idea what time Lawson will be home tonight, so it's 'chippers' for tea. My babies deserve every opportunity for happiness. I can't wait for him to come home. I'm ready to tell him all about Hector and have him help me through however many days I've got left.

After the children went to bed, I waited patiently for our weekly shopping order to be delivered. I was wondering if this would be the last time I'd complete this mundane task? The order this week is bigger than normal as I'm hoping to do some batch cooking on Sunday. Leaving with a freezer well-stocked is another final thing I can do to make whatever is coming easier for Lawson and the kids.

Saturday 16 April

It's 3.24am and I've been awake since I've no idea when.

I'm sitting in the garden with Beau fast asleep beside me.

Utter emptiness – that's what I'm feeling.

I'm struggling to even write, breathe, blink, or exist.

Nothingness.

Yet, there is still an ache emanating from my heart.

Lawson came home last night and woke me up. I was so happy to see him, to be able to finally tell him what's going on. Tell him everything. When he tore my world apart by uttering, "I want a divorce."

All my fears…

All those imaginings…

They all became truths at that moment.

There was nothing I could say in response – nothing.

So, I scraped an ounce of decorum, said "Good night", and turned over. Silent tears began to fall.

He left the bedroom, but came back a while later, got into bed and was asleep almost instantly.

I got up, checked on my babies and came downstairs and

have been here ever since.

More tears have left me. It felt initially that my world was crumpling around me, and I knew I couldn't possibly tell Lawson about Hector. I know I have made mistakes and I am many things, but I am not a person who will ever trap someone with guilt.

I take full responsibility for my actions and the failure of my marriage.

I've failed to be the person that I vowed to become over recent months. I've been remiss in taking an interest in my husband, his work, his hobbies, his life. I haven't even asked him how he is lately!

I've become quite selfish since meeting Hector.

Or more self-focused?

But how do I explain that I never meant to be selfish? I never meant to move away from him. I never meant to not see him as he really is. How do I explain how truly, truly sorry I am without making him feel obliged to remain in our marriage?

Our marriage. Our wonderful colourful marriage.

When we stood in the church on that beautiful May day, the sun streaming in, I knew I'd spend my remaining days with Lawson. As I walked down the aisle with Dad on my arm, walking towards Lawson, I was walking towards my future. There was never a single doubt in my mind that marrying Lawson was the right thing to do.

I remember having a conversation with Andy years later

about how he'd had doubts in the weeks leading up to his and Sophie's wedding. We laughed that it must have been some sort of premonition, as they weren't meant to be together, but I never experienced that – ever.

Lawson is my other half, my best friend, my soulmate, my light, my dark, my colour, my everything. Thanks to him I am the mother of two beautiful babies whom I will treasure until my last breath.

But what can I do?

I can allow him to leave, as he wants.

I could scream at him that he's so very wrong.

No. I don't like confrontation, ever.

I could help him realise that he wants to stay.

Yes?

How?

Sex?

No!

Be realistic, Ann – that isn't something I'm capable of doing right now.

Buy something for him?

God no! Buying people isn't right.

Loving him?

YES!

How?

Love him. Show him I love him. That we love him. That he has a family, and we adore him and want him.

How?

Letter?

Poem?

Song? God no!!!

Food?

YES!!!!

Food!

How?

I need time…

How do I get time?

We won't need the horrific trauma of a divorce if I can gain a few weeks…!

The kids…they are the most important…

Agree but say not yet?

Yes

Ok…

I'll agree but tell him he has to wait a month before telling the children or anyone else.

A lot can happen in a month, can't it?

People fall in love.

People can remember what really matters to them.

People can die.

A month. That's it! A month is all I need.

If I can encourage Lawson to wait a month, everything will be different.

Most importantly I will do everything in my power to

allow Lawson to remember his family, to see the colour in our marriage again.

~

I'm watching the kids wolf down their treat breakfast of waffles and fresh pineapple. They are very content in each other's company. Thankfully, any sibling fighting is limited to who gets to hold the TV remote.

Sitting together at the dining table has always been a big part of our family. It's precious, it's important. It's probably the only time of day when we all stop what we are doing and are together.

THAT'S IT!!!!

I'll agree to Lawson's request for a divorce if he waits a month, and in that month, he comes home from work on time and sits down with us at the dining table and we eat as a family.

I will not guilt my husband into remaining in our family; I'll just remind him what he's been missing.

Remind him to talk to us.

Remind him to laugh with us.

Remind him to love us again.

I texted Mum and asked if she can have the kids to sleep tonight – I didn't tell her why, and she didn't ask. It's never a hardship for Nanny and Grampy to have their mini mess makers.

I've just written a note and left it against the fruit bowl as Lawson's still asleep, telling him I'd be back soon.

Dear Lawson,

I have taken the kids to my folks where they'll have a sleepover tonight.

    I feel it is important that the next few hours to come we are free to be ourselves and not distracted, to talk freely, openly and honestly.

    I will be home around lunchtime.

    I have given your request a lot of thinking and ask that we say nothing to our children at the moment.

    I will graciously and quietly grant your wish for a divorce.

    I do not want anything from you, Rob, not the house, or money. The children will spend their time equally between us but I ask for one condition.

    My condition is:

    You delay proceedings for 30 days, and each of those 30 days you eat dinner with your family at the dining room table – no excuses.

    Annie

~

The kids were so excited when Nanny told them Uncle Andy would be over soon to take them to the cinema! Uncle Andy can do no wrong ever in the eyes of my two, and I dread to think how much sugar they will all consume on this little outing. But

I feel happy knowing they are all having a wonderful time.

When I got home, I struggled to get out of the car, the pain was consuming my body, but I pushed through, limiting myself to just one of the possible two painkillers I can take at a time. They make me sleepy and now is not a time to sleep.

The plan I'd formulated on my drive home fell to bits as soon as I walked through the door. Lawson looked completely confused. So, I just asked him what he'd like for dinner and set about making it.

Cooking and preparing food has always been a way of focusing my mind; it allows me to straighten my thoughts, slows my racing mind and gives me time to get everything lined up in my head. So, I cracked on with making a cottage pie.

In my heart, I know he must be really confused by my response. Did he expect me to shout at him? To hit him? To walk out?

I couldn't ever do any of those things. I loved him.

However...

I had to deal with the elephant in the room.

I know for certain there is another woman in his life.

I take full responsibility for his need and desire and want with looking elsewhere for the simple things I should have been giving him over the past few months.

I let him down.

I let myself down.

I let our marriage down.

I'm so truly sorry.

So, while we were both sitting at the table eating, Lawson with gusto, and me pushing the lovely food around my plate, I knew it was time to face that elephant head-on.

"How was your trip?"

He was confused. His eyes kept shifting left and right, clearly trying to read my face.

"It was a long week with long days. But it was successful. I think we made real progress. They even commented that they think we're now ahead of schedule. I suggested modifying Sub Section 2 for the more environmentally accepted DonMite product and it was a big hit."

Here's where I focused down on my plate of food, and took a big deep breath as a wave of pain washed over my body. I needed to do this. I needed this to be out in the open so that we could move forward. When he'd finished talking about the turbulence I opened my mouth and walked straight into the place of no return.

"Did she enjoy it?" I put a mouthful of the rich food into my mouth and began chewing.

He choked!

He actually choked on his food, he was that shocked!

"I'm not blind, Rob! There was a time when I could make your face light up! I suspect though that those days are now behind us!"

I've built this up into something more than it actually is. It's hard, yes – but it has to be dealt with.

I took another mouthful of food. He never answered me.

That's more telling than giving someone an answer, isn't it?

Fine, I'll be the grown-up, then.

"I simply ask that you don't discuss her within this house, and especially when the children are around. I don't want her to be present 'physically' or any other 'ly' at our dinner table or within this house – ever."

That was it. That's all I had to say on the matter. I don't feel I need to say anything else. He's made his decisions and choices, and I am now choosing how I respond.

I'm choosing to respond with a calm, rational head.

Lawson just sat staring at me, open-mouthed.

"Come on, eat your food. It'll go cold."

I have strength to fight Hector.

I have strength to fight for my marriage.

I don't have strength to fight an unknown person who thinks she can take away my family.

I loaded the dishwasher, cleaned the kitchen down and then went and soaked my aching muscles in a hot bubble bath.

My arms hardly had the energy to lift me out of the tub. I need to sleep.

I need to sleep…

So I can fight…

I honestly thought Lawson would try to talk to me again this evening, but he didn't. Less than twenty-four hours of silence is telling me he wants a divorce and nothing else. He hasn't even acknowledged my note or agreed to my condition.

I've never done divorce before – is this how it happens for other couples?

Sunday 17 April

I think the birds woke me. It was beautiful, so peaceful and calming.

I sat in the conservatory with Beau for company, as I drank my coffee and watched the sunrise.

How had my life come to this? I never envisaged that Lawson and I would become so separated as individuals that our marriage would be at risk.

I never realised I'd have to leave them all so soon.

I need my babies.

I've just texted Mum saying I'm on my way to collect them.

I just need them close.

~

My babies are home, and chaos has descended!

The drive to my parents in Bewdley was just what I needed, surprisingly. I had the windows down and the wind rushed through my hair. I felt more settled by the time I arrived at Mum and Dad's.

Mum took me aside when I got there and said I looked

awful – well, what she said was "peaky".

"More foundation and concealer, sweetie," she said as she embraced me in a big hug.

I managed to grunt my way through making a roast lamb dinner for everyone. The spasms of pain weren't as strong as yesterday, but when they come, they take my breath away.

Lawson ate dinner with us. We all sat around the dining table just like a normal family – but we're not a normal family, are we?

My marriage is falling apart.

My body is falling apart.

My heart is falling apart.

I need to get a grip.

~

I haven't uttered a word about Lawson's request for a divorce since yesterday. I'm not sure how I'm meant to act. Do you discuss it? Do you ignore it? Is it the focus of every conversation you have with your spouse?

YES! I know I said that yesterday!!!!!

I feel very alone, and very confused.

Monday 18 April

I'm so blessed to have been given two wondrous children. On our way to school this morning Lexie started talking to Louis about their favourite foods. It's so lovely to listen to them chatting away to each other.

"Mummy, can we have pizza-off tonight?" Lexie asked.

"What's a 'pizza-off', sweetheart?" I looked at her smiling in the rear-view mirror, knowing exactly what a 'pizza-off' is!!

"You know, Momma, like the Bake Off but with pizza. We each design and make our own pizza. Winner takes the crown!"

They both then proceeded to give me a shopping list of ingredients.

"I can't wait to see what you'll create, Mummy!" Louis said.

"What about Daddy's creation?" I added.

"Daddy won't be there. He's never there when we have dinner," my beautiful little boy said. He wasn't sad about it; he was just stating what he knew to be true. His daddy was never home for things that mattered.

My heart ached for this little boy that had come to live a life where it was normal for his daddy not to be at home.

It's not normal, though, is it?

One side of the table is a husband who wants to divorce his wife.

On the other side of the table is a wife who's being eaten alive.

I texted Lawson when I got back into the car from dropping the kids into school and told him what the kids had suggested for tea. I asked if he'd like to join in and, if so, what ingredients he'd like.

He responded!

He said what ingredients he'd like!

I sat in the car and cried. I cried with joy, happiness, and loss. I'm leaving them and I don't want to.

After nipping to the local shop for all the provisions I'm now back home and waiting for Dr Pacey to visit – wish me luck!

~

Hmmmmm…

Well, that was bloody miserable!

Dr Pacey is a wonderful GP and has become a great source of strength to me over the past few weeks; I shall be eternally grateful to him. However, there really isn't any way of making light or enjoyable the fact that with each passing day I'm coming ever closer to the end.

As he was leaving, he looked up at me and said, "I'm so deeply sorry, Annie. I just wish I had a magic wand. Things like this shouldn't happen to wonderful people like you." Then he left.

What would we all give for a magic wand?

Pre-Hector, would I have waved it for:

A bigger house?

No doubt?

A better job?

No debt?

A bigger car?

A nicer holiday?

Better health…that's the one for me!

Me – Post-Hector:

Time…

Just more time…

~

The pizza-off was a great success.

Lawson was home on time as promised, and seemed to really enjoy the whole process, although he was a little unsure when he first got home. Almost like he didn't know whether to talk to me or not.

I'm pleased to report that Louis James Lawson was crowned the victor with a scrumptious yet disgusting-sounding tuna, pepper, ham, and sweet chilli creation. He's even gone to sleep clutching his own quickly drawn trophy.

My pain hasn't been too bad today. I'm trying to appreciate the moments when it isn't too consuming.

Tuesday 19 April

I spoke too soon, didn't I! The pain has been bad today. I called Mum on the drive back from the school run. I'm struggling to do even the simplest jobs around the house.

I've just had one painkiller and some toast, so hopefully that'll help. I'm just going to lie down on the sofa and wait for Mum to arrive.

~

I must have fallen asleep because when I woke up, I found Mum mopping the bathroom floor singing along to the local radio station!

I helped with the dusting upstairs, as the sleep has done me good.

I really enjoyed just pottering in companionable silence.

When we had finished, I got the kettle on for a well-earned cuppa, when Mum open the oven door and produced a sponge cake. I must have been asleep longer than I'd realised!

As we sat and drank (and ate), we had a good natter, and I dug deep and asked for help – again.

"Mum, I don't know if I'm going to have the strength, or time, to wrap all the presents for the kids."

"Already done, sweetie. I wasn't going to let you tackle such a big job like that! Your dad and I have been wrapping a bit the last few nights. There are only a few more to go. Your dad's loved it! Think I'll get him to wrap this Christmas's presents this year!"

I couldn't help it. The tears just fell from me.

I wasn't going to be here for Christmas.

I wasn't going to be here for Lexie's next birthday.

I wasn't going to be here to see Louis start school.

Will I be here for our next wedding anniversary? Will there even be a reason to celebrate it?

I wasn't going to be here for any of it.

Mum just held me tight as I was racked by wave and wave of unimaginable grief. Grieving for my own death.

My wonderful mum held me so that I didn't break. But I know, as I sit in bed and write this, that it's Mum that's breaking, and I can't stop it.

After I'd pulled myself together, she told me to go and have a soak in the bath while she prepared our dinner.

When I came down, she'd left, and on the dining table was a big bunch of daffodils and a note:

My beautiful baby girl.

I hope your bath has helped ease your muscles.

Dinner is in the oven. You only need to cook the spaghetti. Cheese is grated in the fridge, and I've boxed the cake up for pudding!

Please know how truly loved you are, my angel. How much joy you have brought to my and your father's lives. We adore you and are so proud of everything you've accomplished.

Never feel you've failed, or you are letting us down. You, my angel, are our light, our sun, our moon, our reason for being, and we will shift our orbit to our little cherubs when the time comes.

Stay with us for as long as YOU need to, but not a second longer.

We love you Annie Bear.

Mummy

~

Well, I couldn't write anything after that, sorry, Journal! My mummy sure does know how to make me cry!

But back to today. I hadn't heard anything from Lawson all day, but I'm not concerned. I've been too busy being a blubbery snotty mess!

Dinner was another success. Lawson was home in time and helped me shower Louis – fully clothed afterwards! I don't even want to know how he managed to get spaghetti down his trousers!

It was precious to listen to our little boy inform his daddy why he's SOOOOOOOOOOOO wrong and a T-Rex definitely didn't have purple skin.

I've climbed into bed straight after putting the kids down. I'm aching tonight, not pain, just aching. Let's hope a good night's sleep will help.

Wednesday 20 April

I was too tired last night to write about my visit from Dr Pacey after Mum left. It resulted in my pain meds being increased. So, I'm off to the pharmacy this morning to pick up the prescription – yay, more bloody pills!

I told him that I need something that will just take the edge off the pain, but I don't want to become a zombie. Just block out the worst and I'll deal with the other stuff.

Simon, the pharmacist, is very kind. Whenever I go into cash in a new script he always jokes – "Right, what's today's pick 'n' mix choice!" I'm pretty sure he knows I'm not well – he must do. He is the pharmacist after all, but he's had the good grace never to pry.

~

Dr Pacey has just left. He said I need to be ready. It won't be long now.

Am I ready?

When I think about everyday practical things, I think yes. In my head, everything is organised and sorted, or as much as it can be. Everything is clean, ironed, dusted; the fridge is stocked, and the freezer is crammed with batch-cooked delights. My personal papers are sorted, organised and up to date. Everything I can think of – appointments, clubs, birthdays and activities – is written on the kitchen calendar.

When I think about the people I love, whom I will leave behind, no I am not ready. How can anyone ever be ready to leave the people who bring love, light and magic into their lives?

I simply do not want to leave them.

My babies need their mummy, and I need them.

The kids were both touchy this morning. I know that's my fault. I got them up late, then we had to rush! Which meant lots of Mummy nagging!

So, to make up for a rubbish morning, I promised them their favourite tea – bangers and mash. They both love making mash castles.

~

Tea was a success; all was forgiven and two-and-a-half new castles were built and demolished! Lawson was home on time again. I'm so happy that he's agreed to my condition. He was even belly laughing with the kids when they mocked his attempt at a mash castle. It was heart-warming to see.

Unfortunately, a wave of pain shot through my body just as I sat down at the table and Lawson noticed me wince. I just said I was tired – which is true, just not the whole truth.

He offered to run me a bath after we'd cleaned the dinner things away and the kids were asleep. It was so unexpected, yet something my husband of old would do. Is he coming back to us?

Please forgive me, Lawson. Please forgive my half-truths. Please forgive me for not being able to fight this well enough. Please forgive me for having a body that didn't work like it's supposed to. Please forgive me for leaving.

Hector has been on my mind a lot today. Not in terms of me, but of the impact it will have on the kids. Louis and Lexie are going to have to grow up without their mother standing beside them. Their little worlds are going to implode in the not-too-distant future. How will my leaving impact their futures – the choices they make, the relationships they forge?

I've pondered death far too much over the past few weeks. Would it be better for a person's death to be sudden – no warning? Or is it better to know it's coming?

What about the impact on those who are left behind? Is it easier to watch your loved one die? You can prepare yourself. Or is it better to have no knowledge of what's to come?

The conclusion I came to, my deepest wish from all of this, is to somehow protect them from the hurt that is going to crash over them. I know it will happen. I also know I can't stop it, but I wish with my every fibre that I could.

Thursday 21 April

Day six in the post-divorce world and I feel like I'm starting to accept and forgive myself and Lawson for ballsing it all up.

We've both cocked up majorly, haven't we?

We all make mistakes, we're only human. It's what we do, once we realise we've messed up, that defines us as individuals.

Blimey, that's a bit profound for 6.30am!

~

Dr Pacey has just left, and he is now carrying my envelope with him in his briefcase and has taken to asking me if there's anything I'd like to add. No, there isn't anything, but I've been thinking about the letter I need to write to Lawson. This book is good, but it's not enough, is it?

But then how does one go about writing a final letter to the person they've chosen to spend the rest of their life with?

Every single couple goes through ups and downs throughout their relationship. Right now we're on a downward slope – no we're not, we're climbing back up the hill.

Lawson said he wants to divorce – is that because that's the easy way out or because that is what he wants to do?

I'm not naive enough to presume what another person wants, let alone the person closest to me. All I can do is know exactly what I want – and that's my husband and my wonderful family.

I think a letter may be a good idea, but I need to prepare myself! I don't have time on my side, so perhaps I just need to pull my big-girl pants on and be brave again?

Mum arrived just as the doctor was leaving and between the three of us, we managed to carry all the wrapped presents into the house. I made room at the bottom of my wardrobe. Mum got inside, beneath the clothes, and I passed them down to her.

We both sat on the floor and stared at our handiwork. I knew it was time to say goodbye to my wonderful mummy. I turned to face her and took hold of her hand.

"Mum, don't be sad I'm going. Be joyous that I've lived, and I have lived! I've been so blessed with a happy love-filled life. You and Daddy gave me so much – a wonderful start, and a fantastic example of how to be a good parent. I couldn't have asked for more."

She began to cry and smile at the same time.

"I love you, Mum."

~

The walk home from school was fantastic. Both the kids were

in a good mood, and in between bug hunting, shadow hopping and an intense session of I spy, we decided that we should have enchiladas for dinner tonight.

Lawson arrived home earlier than normal – which was a wonderful surprise for the kids, but I must confess it threw me a bit! He even offered to help me make the food!

Is he enjoying being at home with us? Is he enjoying having dinner with us? He's smiling again, talking with me, not shouting at the kids.

I don't dare to hope too much. Hope is reserved for those with time. Hope is tied to longevity, not those short on time.

I called Andy after Mum left earlier and said a final goodbye. Just Dad left now, and he's going to be the hardest of the three of them. Then it's Lawson and my beautiful babies.

Even if I do it and don't leave for another week, at least I got to tell them all exactly how much they mean to me. If only I could tell them how truly terrified I am. Not of dying! I'm not scared of that. I'm utterly petrified of leaving them.

Friday 22 April

I'm struggling today. I've already had more pain medication than I normally do. I've got sharp stabbing pains that don't seem to be easing.

Dr Pacey is on his way.

Lawson just texted saying he'll collect the kids from school today, which I'm amazed at. He never normally collects them. He never usually leaves work early!

But it does mean I can rest, and possibly nap without worrying about the school run.

When I look back over our life together, I know with absolute certainty that I made the right decision to marry Lawson. I knew in my very soul that he would be an amazing father. Our children have total command of that man's heart (and wallet!). I do NOT regret a single day of our relationship, not even one.

~

Thankfully, Dr Pacey's visit today was short as he is on call for his practice. He gave me that 'knowing look' all over again!

I told him I'd planned to get some sleep once he left.

~

Chippers for tea! The kids and Lawson came home with fish and chips, and we had a treat-night eating it in front of the TV. Something so simple can really make your soul smile, can't it?

I'm glad Louis devoured his and asked for more, as I was able to slide most of my meal onto his plate. At least it didn't look like I hadn't eaten then!

I feel rough. I'm trying not to show it. But it's tough.

Saturday 23 April

Sunday 24 April

Yesterday was the worst I've felt. So much pain really is debilitating. I was crawling to the bathroom, but even that made me feel sick – constantly.

Lawson saw me throwing up yesterday. Thankfully, he thinks it was the fish from Friday night.

He totally took over – the kids, the house, the cooking, even Beau. He was amazing. I am so lucky that he is a good daddy.

I feel better today – totally drained, but the pain is under control, and I've only had one of the pain meds.

When I finally woke up at 11am, the house was quiet, and Beau was asleep in her cage. After a refreshing pint of ice-cold water, a shower, and some fresh clothes I feel halfway to feeling human.

I cooked a roast chicken for everyone, and we had warm chicken salad for tea as the kids told me they'd had something to eat while out with Daddy. They were so animated when they told me about their adventures.

I'm in bed already and it's only 7.25pm. I'm about to turn the lights off and get my head down.

Monday 25 April

It's been a busy morning. I got home from the school run to find Lawson was walking down our road, clearly taking Beau for a walk.

I wound down the window and pulled the car to a stop.

"What are you doing here?" I leant my arm on the window ledge.

"I've called in sick. I'm going to take Beau for a long walk. I think the girl deserves a bit of a run about!" He scratched her ears.

"You're sick? Are you ok? Do you need me to phone the doctor?" He can't be ill! We've only enough room for one of us being poorly.

"I... I... I'm tired, Ann. I just want a bit of a rest."

"Well, I think that sounds great. You deserve a rest – make sure you do just that! I'll see you two later."

As I carried on up the road and up to our drive, I hit the call button on my mobile and called the GP surgery. I must make sure Dr Pacey doesn't come to the house today.

~

I ended up visiting the surgery to see Dr Pacey. He checked my blood pressure, which was a bit on the low side, so he told me to rest.

I went straight to school after the appointment and when we got home, we walked into a house full of delicious smells.

Lawson had cooked! I was (and still am) genuinely shocked!

Jacket spuds with cold ham and salad.

As we all sat around the dining table, Lawson told me that he was going to be taking the week off work.

Shit!

Instant selfishness swept through me. His being here interferes with the doctor's visits, naps and taking meds.

But my rational head kicked in seconds later. He deserves a break. He does work so hard for all of us.

I just needed reasons (many reasons) why I wouldn't be home a lot of the time.

'I'm dying' doesn't really cut it!

I encouraged him to try to rest this week and take Beau out for lots of walks; that always calms him down. And hopefully recharge his batteries.

Tuesday 26 April

I agreed to meet Mum and Dad today. It was time to talk to my fabulous father.

Wonderful Dad, a bit what people might call 'old fashioned' but totally marvellous all the same. Dad is and always has been set in his ways. He's very 'black and white', not even a hint of grey.

That said, he's Dad and an amazing Grampy.

Lawson is being very attentive, although he seems distant. However, we are all enjoying having him home for a bit.

He even offered to take the kids to school this morning, which meant that I could get to the doctor's before seeing Mum and Dad.

I'm in the waiting room now, looking around at the variety of people sitting waiting patiently for their turn.

That's all life is really, isn't it? Waiting for your turn. Waiting for your turn to see the doctor. Waiting for your turn at the checkout. Waiting for your turn at the traffic lights. Waiting for your turn to die.

The weather was bloody awful all day. I came home looking and feeling like a drowned rat!

The overwhelming message again from Dr Pacey was to rest – which I have to say is easier said than done when you have small children, even if you are dying!

Being a mummy is something I've always dreamed of. Baking with them, cuddling them, making a mess with them, loving them – my whole being is for them, every beat of my heart is for them.

Moving on to Dad…

Dad was – so dad-like!

"Dad, come on." I grabbed hold of his elbow. "Come and show me how your roses are getting on," I said, as we walked out of the house and up into his immaculate garden. Borders on either side of the path will be awash with colour in the coming weeks and all the way through until October. Dad has always had green fingers, passed on by his dad, apparently.

"I thought I'd lost this one last month, but she seems to be fighting back." He bent to touch the leaves of one of his roses.

"Dad?" He carried on inspecting the lower leaves. "Daddy!"

"The leaves are looking so much better," he added. He hadn't even heard me!

"Daddy! Please! I need to do this now, and I need you to listen to me." I took a deep breath as he stood up and looked at me.

"Ann, love, what's the matter?" He looked so worried.

"I need to…" A single tear fell down my face. "To say goodbye, Daddy, and to tell you that I love you."

His eyes became watery, and he embraced me in an all-consuming hug. "Oh, my baby girl." And he held me tight. "I love you, too. I remember holding you for the first time after you were born. You held on so tight to my finger, and I looked at you and thought how absolutely perfect you were." He released me from the hug, his face awash with tears. "And I look at you now and you're still perfect."

I stifled a laugh.

"Ann, darling, we will never let Rob feel he's on his own, not ever. We will sweep them all up and hold them tight and love them until they're ready to walk on their own."

~

Lawson made dinner again tonight – all by himself! He seems happy, a lot less stressed. As we sat down to a plateful of homemade fish pie, Lawson asked if we could go out together tomorrow after dropping the kids off at school.

Why does he want to go out?

What does he want us to do?

Does he want to talk?

Is he going to tell me he doesn't want to agree to my condition anymore?

What does he want?

Oh, God!

Wednesday 27 April

Another day...

Ive been gifted another day...

Every single day counts...

Every single hour counts...

Every single minute counts...

Make it count...

Breakfast was so relaxed. We all sat at the dining table, the conservatory doors wide open, and had a great time, everyone chatting, laughing and happy. Beau darting in and out of the garden, barking happily at birds and insects.

We had the tunes blasting out in the car as we drove the kids to school.

Lawson asked me where I'd like to go once we were back in the car. There's only one place I want to go when the sun's out and the clouds have disappeared.

The Boat Shack...

The feeling of space that comes from sitting on the deck looking out over the water – there's nowhere quite like it.

I am tired today.

I am tired of holding everything together.

I'm tired of being positive.

I'm tired of being upbeat.

I'm tired of having to fight.

I'm tired of being tired.

I knew I was going to cry.

We got to the lake so early that Karen the owner was only just setting up for the day. I am so grateful to her for her discretion when she saw me arrive with Lawson. She didn't give anything away about our conversation a few days ago.

After grabbing a couple of warm blankets, we settled at one of the tables on the decking overlooking the lake, which surprisingly already had a few brave swimmers embarking on chilly laps around the open water.

There was only one question I wanted to be answered before we left. One thing I needed to know.

"Are you still seeing HER?" I tried to hold my voice steady; it was a struggle.

His response took the wind from me.

"Yes."

My dam collapsed with that one word. Everything that I've been holding so tightly to just crumbled away.

Perhaps there was a small hope within me that it might have been a one-off? He's never going to see her again.

I want my husband. I want my family.

I need my family.

He then turned in his chair to face me as he said that, however, he hadn't seen her since last week.

So, she worked with him.

Check!

At least that explains Berlin.

We drank our hot chocolate in relative silence.

Lawson tried to apologise for his behaviour.

I just didn't have the energy to fight, or even talk about it. I felt utterly drained.

I needed to go home. I texted Dr Pacey on our way home, cancelling my appointment today. I reassured him I was 'OK-ish', just going home to go to bed. I needed to sleep.

Thursday 28 April

I slept solidly for four hours yesterday when we got home. I only woke up when Lex and Lou arrived home and kissed me awake to tell me they'd brought dinner on a tray and that we were going to snuggle in the bed and eat together.

It was fantastic.

Lawson made kebabs. I picked at the food while the kids devoured it down like they'd never been fed.

I, however, devoured them. Watching the three of them interacting, laughing, smiling, telling each other stories.

God, I love them so much.

The kids and I must have dropped off to sleep, all snuggled up in the bed. I woke up about 1.30am to find Louis star-fishing across the whole bed, Lex holding on tightly to me and no sign of Lawson.

What a gloriously messy way to wake up with the sun, surrounded by my beautiful babies.

Another memory made, without even trying.

Perhaps waking up with my babies contributed to how I feel this morning. I feel – good.

After taking the kids into school and covering them with kisses I went straight to the doctor, where he gave me that 'knowing' look. I know my good days are going to be few and far between as Hector gets a tighter grip on my body.

I'm currently sitting in the car park at the doctor's as I write this – composing myself, as I know Lawson will be home when I get back. Hopefully, I'll appear nearly normal.

There was a text message waiting for me when I came out of the appointment. It was from Janey, asking if she could collect the kids from school.

Of course you can, they'll be so thrilled. Why don't you come back for dinner with us?

I instantly texted Lawson.

Your mum has just messaged asking if she can collect the kids from school. I said yes, of course she can and asked if she'd like to stay for dinner. It will be nice to see her.

He's just responded:

Sounds like a plan, Batman. Let's order a pizza delivery.

I put my phone down and turned on the car engine and another message came through from Lawson.

I miss you

I turned the engine off, as I sobbed, ungraceful, undignified, and ugly sobbing. My husband misses me. I miss him. I don't want to leave him. He's coming back to me, just as I'm preparing to leave him.

Shitting fucking HECTOR.

FUCK YOU, HECTOR.

~

Dinner was a glorious mixture of pizza, garlic dough balls and laughter.

Janey stayed to put the kids to bed, which they both loved, as Nan does the best voices for bedtime stories apparently.

My wonderful mother-in-law is a port in any storm and always has been. I know she will steer Lawson and the kids once I've gone. I know she will sweep them up just like my mum and dad and love them hard.

I feel tired tonight, but not exhausted tired, just a busy day tired.

Oh, and I'd like to take this opportunity to apologise for my language earlier. Swearing does not become me. I promise it won't happen again.

Friday 29 April

Lawson has taken the kids to school. He said he'd got a few things to do in town so would be back about 10am-ish and cook us breakfast. So, I called the GP surgery and asked for Dr Pacey's home visit to be cancelled today.

SOD

SODDING IT

SOD IT SODDING

WHAT

THE

ACTUAL

She was here!

Her!

She was in my house!

The absolute cheek!!!!!!!!!!!!!!!!!!!

She came to my front door.

She rung my door bell!

She was here!

She was in my house – the fucking cheek of the woman.

I knew exactly who she was when I opened the front door, and she introduced herself.

"I'm Bex Green. I work with Rob. Is he home?" she announced while leaning up against the door frame, and looking over my shoulders into my house.

I genuinely can't believe the nerve to turn up at my house! She didn't care! The selfishness of her!

He's not even in work! He'd agreed with them to have this week as annual leave.

However, my politeness kicked in (bloody parents!). I'll be having words with them about installing such manners in me!

"Come through into the kitchen. He'll be home soon. He's taking OUR children to school."

I was about to question why this woman thought it was acceptable to come to my home when Lawson opened the front door. We could hear him humming to himself. He walked into the kitchen carrying the biggest bunch of beautiful flowers.

I was shocked, surprised and saddened. Another bunch of flowers that were going to outlive me! Then I was angry with myself for being saddened about such an irrelevant thing at this important time!

After grabbing a vase, I went into the living room to arrange them, giving them room to discuss whatever it was that was SOOOOOOO important.

I'm not ashamed to say I was listening at the door the whole time, the beautiful flowers dumped on the coffee table.

I could hear Lawson's anger as he tried to whisper.

However – what I am ashamed of is…what happened after I heard that little bitch utter these words:

"To tell your wife maybe?"

My blood just boiled.

I'm not one for confrontation – I don't even massively like swearing – but my God, something took over me.

I walked confidently back into MY kitchen, ignoring her. I couldn't look at her. I wrapped my arms around Lawson, using his strength. I finally looked her square in the eyes and simply said:

"She already knows! Next?"

Again, shame creeps over me now as I recall what I did next.

I am sorry, really, I am.

But I laughed at her.

I didn't mean to.

I've always hated people who belittle others, bully them, or even try to shame them.

She stared between the both of us, shifting her feet. Clearly deciding her next move. However, what she told us was totally unexpected. We couldn't have foreseen it. Lawson's boss, David Morris, had died.

It was just bloody awful.

But there's more – he'd left Morris and Co to Lawson.

~

I just couldn't carry on writing.

It's such a shock.

It's unbelievable.

First, David is gone. His poor wife, Sheila. I'm going to try to give her a call tomorrow. David was such a lovely man. He cared so much for Lawson; he guided and encouraged him every day that he worked for him. Lawson often told me that David would always ask after me and the kids. We'd been invited to their house on numerous occasions, a summer barbecue and a lovely Christmas party, mainly for the children as Sheila and David had no children of their own. I caught David watching the children playing on his pristine lawn last summer at the barbecue and asked him what he was thinking.

"You can have bucketfuls of success, Annie. You can have bank accounts overflowing. But when it all comes down to it, does any of it matter? Look at those two innocent and precious little souls. That's all Sheila and I ever wanted, you know? To have our own children, but it never happened. No amount of money or influence helped. It just was never meant to be."

"I'm sorry to hear that, David. Had you not considered adopting?" I asked.

"Oh, gosh, Ann, we've considered absolutely everything – adoption, fostering, surrogacy. Unfortunately, we always seemed to stall committing to anything for we both had an unwavering hope that things would happen naturally. Unfortunately, we ran out of time and were suddenly classed as 'too old'!" He chuckled. "I mean we didn't even know we'd got a clock ticking away in the background!"

"Oh, David, I'm so sorry." I consoled him by putting my hand on his arm.

"Treasure them, Annie. Always treasure them," he said.

Second, that he's left the business to Lawson. It changes everything – massively.

After that woman stormed out of the house, I knew Lawson was going into shock. So I grabbed him as he slumped to the floor, devastation and grief claiming him.

We got him dressed and he is now on his way to the office to speak to Sheila.

~

I still can't believe it!

I've just realised that I've been in the living room for twenty minutes staring into space without even realising it!

I called Mum and Dad after Lawson left and told them what was happening.

It's just such a shock.

~

Lawson didn't get home for dinner tonight, and he was clearly upset about that fact when he did get back.

We sat in the conservatory after the kids had gone to sleep and he told me all about David's wishes.

He is so nervous, scared, worried, unsure, and frankly marvellous. He will be an outstanding boss, a fabulous leader, and a great example for our children.

"What the hell am I going to do, Ann? What the hell are WE going to do?" He struggled to get his words out.

I grabbed both his hands in mine and looked him square in the face. "You listen to me, ROBERT. You're going to go into that office tomorrow morning. You'll talk to the staff and reassure them, because they are all going to be devastated, confused and probably fearful for their jobs. Then you will come home and play football in the back garden with your son. Probably lose a colouring competition with your daughter. Climb into bed tomorrow night and hold me tight as you drift off to sleep knowing how truly loved you are, Lawson, because we do love you. I love you."

I felt a release as I expressed how I truly felt. I love Lawson more than I've ever loved anyone. I needed him to know, in that moment, that I love him.

It wasn't a goodbye, it was…reaffirming my love and unwavering support for him.

"None of this could have been foreseen. This isn't what we'd planned. None of this could have been planned."

I feel… How do I feel about this change in circumstance?

I don't know!

Selfishly, I feel that it'll take him further away from me physically, right now, and I need him. But he doesn't even know that I need him because I'm a bloody coward and can't tell him that I've failed at the simplest task – living.

How will this change impact Lawson once I'm gone?

How will it impact the children?

It's certainly going to take more of his time; he's the boss now!

Will he want to be the boss?

Does he want this responsibility?

What can I do?

Nothing!

No, I can be his wife.

I can support him.

I can make sure he looks after himself when he's here. I'll make sure he's got food with him. Lots of cuddles when he gets home, and as much reassurance as I can possibly give.

This isn't fighting. This is doing what I'm best at – being his wife.

It's the job I was born to do.

It's what I vowed to do all my life.

To be Lawson's wife...

Not sure either of us got much sleep last night. Lawson was tossing and turning all night. I, on the other hand, was experiencing random shooting pains across my stomach.

I got up in the night to go to the toilet only to find that I was bleeding.

Period?

Something else?

I sent a text message to Dr Pacey, apologising for interrupting his weekend and asking if I need to worry.

~

Lawson left early this morning. He's going to speak to all the Morris and Co staff. He was so worried that he isn't all that they need him to be.

But he is so much more.

He's a capable man who is dedicated to his job.

He's also our everything.

He's everything we've ever needed.

He's our world.

Over breakfast, Louis asked if it was going to be nice today so we could spend it in the garden. I grabbed my phone and we all looked at the weather forecast – wall-to-wall sunshine – and decided the only thing for it was to go to the shops and bring home enough barbecue food to feed the whole street. Lex wrote out the list, while Lou pored over the fridge contents.

Hot dogs…

Burgers…

Chicken pieces…

Chops…

Kebabs…

Giant mushrooms…

Corn on the cobs…

Oh and of course, a French stick, plus whole French sticks just for Louis!

~

We've had such a good time shopping.

Each of the kids had a little trolley with a French stick each, and a tub of ice cream each.

They are currently splashing around in the paddling pool and sliding down the water sheet – they're so happy.

I called Sheila just now while the kids were paddling.

She is totally devastated. Broken.

The poor woman. She didn't even get to say goodbye to him. She said that she's travelled down to their holiday home in

North Devon. I needed to implement my North Devon plan; it's now or never.

"Oh, Annie, how kind of you to call," she said.

"Sheila, I'm so deeply sorry for your loss. I don't even know what to say."

"What can you say, dear? It's just horrific. I keep looking out of the window and across and out to sea. I don't know, Annie, but I've always found staring out to sea brings a sense of fragility into one's life – don't you think?"

"Yes, I do actually." I knew exactly what she meant. "Sheila, I know this isn't the best of times, but I need to ask for your help."

"Oh, my darling girl, there will never be a 'right' time to ask for anyone's help. That's why we must seize the now and make it the time," she said with conviction.

Blimey that was deep!

"Sheila, I'm dying. I have cancer."

I heard her gasp, and then silence.

"Sheila? Sheila? Are you ok? Sheila?"

"Oh, my darling girl!" I heard her say through tears.

"Sheila, it's ok. I've… I've accepted it. Sheila, Rob doesn't know. He doesn't know I'm sick or that I'll be dying. I can't tell him. I can't bear the thought of pity darkening my final days."

"Oh, I understand, my dear. Your final days should be on your own terms," she said with certainty.

"I'm going to ask my mum to call you when…it's happened.

Could Rob and the kids come to you in North Devon for a few days? I've spent some time with Jennifer at The Teacup in the harbour, and I'd love for Rob to visit her after I've gone."

"Oh, Jen is lovely, isn't she? Don't you worry about a thing, Annie, dear; I'll get Rob down here if I have to drive him myself."

"Thank you, Sheila, thank you for your understanding."

"Be brave, my girl, you are a remarkable individual and it's been my pleasure to class you as a friend," Sheila said without a single break in her voice.

"Sheila, the pleasure was all mine. Your strength is remarkable. Thank you for everything. Take care, bye-bye."

Ending the call, I stared across the garden to the children playing on the swing and slide. I know that today's the day I need to say goodbye to my babies and it's breaking my heart.

~

Dr Prescott called this afternoon; Dr Pacey called her after my middle-of-night text. She confirmed what I knew deep down. It's not good.

Bleeding is an indication that the end is not far away.

I really appreciate her honesty with me. She doesn't sugar-coat anything or fluff over her words.

Although she recommended admittance to the hospital, I refused. I'm fine. The pain has subsided now, and although I'm still bleeding, it's just like managing a period.

She did chuckle when I said I wouldn't be going in. "That's

159

exactly what I expected you to say, Annie!"

She ended the call by advising me to just wear pads, monitor the flow, and contact her straight away if it gets any heavier.

~

I said goodbye to Louis first – my gorgeous little heartbreaker in the making.

"Lou…come and sit with Momma a minute." He waddled over to me. Clearly, his pockets were weighed down with precious stones again!

"Hi, Momma. Can we snuggle a second?" He climbed up on my lap.

"Always, mate, we can always snuggle!" I smelled his hair – just perfect. "Mate, I just wanted to tell you how amazing you are, and how much I love you."

"I love you too, Mum. But you know I'm quite busy stone-sorting now!" He looked at me.

"You'll always remember that you are my favourite boy, won't you?" I asked.

"Oh of course, Momma. You've always told me that!"

"I love you, little man, with every bit of my heart." I held him a bit tighter.

"Mummmmmmm. You're squishing me!" He giggled as he wriggled free and waddled back off to the rockery in the corner of the garden.

My little lady was a bit trickier.

"Lex, love, come here, darling." I beckoned her over to me as I pulled my legs up underneath me on the sofa, trying to keep in the shade of the big parasol umbrella.

"Mum, do you think this doll looks better in this outfit or this one?" She held up both outfits.

"Well, they are both beautiful, sweetie. I guess it depends on what the dolly is planning on doing while she wears the outfit."

"They're going for a picnic with my bears," she confirmed.

"Oh well, definitely this one then, darling." I pointed to the flowery dress.

"You're right, Mum." She discarded the other dress on the patio slabs.

"Sweetie, I wanted to talk to you?"

"Oh, ok, Mum, I'll just carry on dressing my dolly though." She didn't look up from unfastening the buttons on the back of the dress.

"Darling, I'm so proud of you. You make my heart smile every day. The day you were born was the happiest of my life. I am so, so happy to be your momma," I said, trying not to let go of the tears that were threatening to fall.

She looked up – mid buttoning. "Momma, I love you and you make me so happy, too." She smiled and then she walked off back to her dolly pram down by the conservatory.

"Don't forget me, kids," I whispered to the wind.

Lawson's meeting went as well as could be expected. Everyone is nervous, grief-stricken and worried.

After we put the children to bed and I was cleaning the kitchen and putting the mountain of leftover barbecue food in the container, he came in and stood in the middle of the room, looking like a lost child, simply. He said, "Annie, please… Please will you hold me?" And tears started to fall.

I held my darling husband as he broke. Safely in my arms. I will never allow him to break – ever.

This wonderful human, my boy, my love.

Sunday 01 May

Another glorious day…

A brand new month dawns…

I'm feeling very melancholy about that…

I will never see the end of this month…

I know this…

This is the month that will always be associated with my death – not my marriage…

I have no fear about dying, just sadness about leaving those I love. I also know I keep saying that – I'm sorry!

Lexie and Louis have no idea that I spent most of yesterday saying goodbye to them.

Holding them both in turn close to my chest. Telling them how treasured they are. Ensuring that they heard that I believe they will make a massive impact on the world and how I WILL ALWAYS be right beside them in whatever they choose to do.

Whispering, over and over again in their ears, that I love them.

Now to say goodbye to Lawson, which is going to be even harder given the fact he doesn't know I'm leaving.

~

I have felt sluggish today. But the meds are definitely taking the edge off the pain.

I successfully made a roast pork dinner for everyone but couldn't face eating it myself. There's something comforting about watching your family tuck into the food you've prepared for them.

Lawson has been quiet all day. He's been hunched over his laptop, trying to get his head around the path before him. I offered to make some shortbread biscuits for him to take into the office. When I say make shortbread biscuits, I mean shortbread splodges as the kids stood up on their respective steps at the counters and 'helped' me make them. There isn't really anything else I can do to show Lawson my support.

Lexie loved helping to roll the mixture out and insisted on cutting some as gingerbread men shapes!!

How many more opportunities will I get to bake with my babies?

So many missed opportunities that I took for granted just a year ago.

Life is so short. Life is so precious. Life is so magical. Never waste a second.

Monday 02 May

Lawson was up early. He wanted to be in the office before anyone else arrived this morning.

I stood on the landing watching as he kissed the kids goodbye.

I know he will raise them well, of that I am certain. He was restless last night, tossing and turning. I tried to soothe him with 'shush' and 'it'll be ok'. Once he'd settled, I spoke to him as he dreamed.

"Lawson, please know that I love you. I don't want to leave you. God! I'm so scared to not physically be by your side, but please know wherever I end up I'll be watching on, so proud of everything you achieve, everything our babies achieve. I'll always love you – never doubt that. You ARE my everything."

Then, when we were both awake and ready for the day, I stood with him at the front door and waved goodbye.

"Good luck, boss! You know it's going to be a tough day, don't you? So, let's accept that, and simply look for the positives in the day." I stroked his arms, reassuringly.

"Thank you, love. I still can't believe it's happening. This time last week I was racked with guilt because I'd pulled a sickie, now I'm the bloody boss!" He threw his arms up in the air.

Pulling his coat around him, I looked him in the face and from the bottom of my heart said, "YOU are the boss. But you're not a tree, Lawson. If you don't like what you're doing, then move! You don't have to stay being a boss if you don't like it." I held on tighter to his coat as a wave of pain rushed through me. "David wouldn't have left the business to you if he didn't think you could handle it. He believed in you. So do I."

He seemed so unsure for a few seconds, then he kissed me and held me in an all-consuming hug.

"I promise I'll be home for dinner," he said.

"My condition is flexible. This is not what we'd planned as a couple or a family. None of this is what we'd ever planned. Poor David. I understand that other things have to come first."

~

Dr Pacey came this morning. We talked about the bleeding, which has slowed now. The occasional wave of pain but nothing constant.

With each visit, I can see more sadness in his eyes. He's such a lovely man.

"I'm going to write Rob a letter to go in the envelope. I'm not quite finished yet, though – well actually, I haven't even started yet!" I told him.

"Whenever you're ready, Annie. I promise he'll receive it." He waved me goodbye.

~

I felt a boost of energy this afternoon. So while we were waiting for the fish fingers to cook, the kids and I had a mini disco in the kitchen. A little boogie to some tunes – just bloody precious.

Lawson, as promised, was home for dinner and is now fast asleep next to me – one arm slung across my stomach and snoring gently.

He wants to be close to me.

He's coming back to me.

I can feel it, and time has run out. It's breaking my heart.

I forgive him wholeheartedly for his time with her. I'm responsible.

Our undying deep-rooted love is all that matters and will always matter.

I love and forgive my darling man.

Tuesday 03 May

Lawson was gone early again this morning. He seems – down? Distant? Distracted? Totally understandable given what's happening.

The weight of the responsibility is clearly weighing on him. I wish I could take that weight off him.

It's funny how when times are tough you never see the opportunity for change and growth while you're in the eye of the storm. You just focus on the immediate impact.

My only wish is that the storm passes quickly.

He told me that David's funeral will take place in a couple of weeks. Poor Sheila. I keep thinking about her and the pain she must be going through all on her own in North Devon. Is she ok? Perhaps being on her own is helpful to her?

~

My visit with Dr Pacey was tough today. There simply isn't any humour or jest left, just a serious tone on how little time I now have left.

Mum and Dad are going to collect the kids today and

possibly, maybe, have a secret visit to 'the restaurant with the big M' as Louis calls it! However, it's all top secret; I'm not to know a thing about it.

I'm still working on Lawson's letter; it's just hard to put into words a lifetime of things I want to say.

~

I have spent most of today resting on the sofa, I feel…weak.

No, not weak…

Weary.

Fighting is hard. I'm realising that I massively underestimated how hard this was going to be.

The kids came home full of giggles and 'definitely not a toy'. Grampy had the joy of bathing them both. He came downstairs looking drenched!

Two-and-a-half bedtime stories, three rounds of I spy later, and the kids are finally fast asleep.

I hugged Mum and Dad tight as I said goodbye to them.

I know.

I know…

I…

I know in my heart I probably won't see them again…

I'm sorry, Mum and Dad.

I'm sorry for the pain you're feeling right now, the pain that is to come. I'm so truly sorry.

But I love you so very much.

Wednesday 04 May

Lawson came home late last night. He was so apologetic that he missed dinner, to which I had the joy of telling him all about 'the secret dinner at the M restaurant'.

We laughed as I sat on the edge of the bath while he soaked his weary muscles.

It was…normal.

Just normal.

Just wonderful.

It's a lovely day today; I think we'll walk to school this morning.

~

After dropping the children off, I headed over to Liv and Zak's for the final time. The walk normally takes two minutes, but my slow-and-steady old-tortoise pace took me nearly twenty minutes.

They are such good friends. When I'm gone, I know Lawson will be cared for.

I think I'll write a letter to Zak; he's going to be one of the main supports Lawson will turn to.

It is lovely to see them both so happy in their marriage. Saying goodbye as I left felt...easy. I know they will be ok.

I made lasagne when I got back. Today has been a good day.

As I sit here, I just re-read some of this book. I've realised that I've been very...leaving heavy!

I don't mean to focus on leaving.

I don't mean to be glum.

I want to focus on staying.

Focus on everything that matters.

Being told your days are numbered allows a sort of peace to wash through your very soul, as well as utter fear and trepidation all at the same time. It allows the important things in life to become focused and the nonsense to slip away.

What matters – truly matters – is your family. The people you love, the people who make your soul sing.

Nothing else has any consequence.

I know I'm loved and yes that matters, but to let the people you are leaving know that you love them is just as important.

~

I spoke to Dr Pacey on the phone as I was sitting in the car waiting to collect the kids. He's going to come tomorrow. He was honest and said that he won't be doing any more tests; he just wanted to perform welfare checks.

The kids inhaled their tea. I have no idea where they put

it all! Hollow legs, Mum used to say, when Andy and I were growing up. I remember our childhood favourite was dinosaur-shaped chicken with trees (broccoli) and Mum's chips – we didn't have them all the time, but God, they were amazing.

Lawson didn't make it home in time for dinner this evening. He looks drawn. I'm sure he's lost weight. This bequest has definitely come with worry and stress. I was going to have a chat with Lawson about how it's going but he fell asleep, looking just like Louis.

Thursday 05 May

Today I am a woman with a plan. Dr Pacey should be here around 1pm. The plan is to have Lawson's letter written and ready for him so it can be added to the envelope.

Last night, I struggled to sleep, so I got up and packed a lunch box full of food for Lawson to take to work. I fixed a note to the top of the box.

One thing at a time, A x.

I also stuck a note to the back of the front door saying 'Fridge'.

I must not have heard him leave as I was woken up by the alarm. His side of the bed was empty and cold. Just like mine will be soon.

The kids were reluctant to leave their beds this morning. But after a little persuasion of chocolate toast, they were up like a shot.

Now to usher them out of the house! Wish me luck.

~

I spent the morning sitting in the study, the sun flooding in, and I felt lighter. Writing Lawson's letter has helped.

5 May

Lawson,

If you are reading this then my time has come to an end. Please don't be sad I'm gone, be happy that I lived.

I know you're going to be angry that I never told you I was ill, but please try to understand my reasons:

1. *I wanted to live a life without pity*
2. *I wanted to live a 'normal' life with you and the children, not consumed with hospital visits and medical appointments*
3. *I wanted to continue to be your wife*
4. *I wanted to continue to be our babies' momma*
5. *I wanted to be more than this illness*
6. *Selfishly I don't think I have the strength to tell you. Every ounce of my energy has been going into fighting, fighting to stay with you all.*

I have pancreatic cancer (which I fondly refer to as Hector!!) – Hector's gotten too big, he's too far gone to be treated. He's S4,

Stage 4, which means he's travelled beyond my pancreas. He's basically spreading throughout my body. I've not been feeling 'right' for a little while, but just put it down to how busy things have been around here lately.

I found out for certain 6 weeks ago! Six weeks ago I was told I'd got six weeks to live, that's how advanced it was (is).

I really did try to find a way to tell you what was happening. I struggled to find the right words to convey that I would be leaving you. I tried every day, but the words just got stuck in my throat. I managed to talk myself into telling you when you came home from Berlin; unfortunately you had other ideas, telling me you wanted a divorce, which if I'm being truthful hurt more than being told my days were literally numbered.

Please know that I take full responsibility for the decline in our relationship over the past few months. I've felt so poorly at times I've simply not been able to fulfil my obligation to you, no, my promise to be your wife, in all senses of the word. Therefore I do not in any way blame you for looking elsewhere.

I'm not angry at you, Lawson. When you asked me for a divorce I wasn't surprised; I was just deeply sorrowful, as I knew eventually it would come. That's why I agreed to your request, but with the addition of my condition.

Why? I know, I can hear your voice even now!

I asked you to wait 30 days before making anything official. Well the reason I asked for that is because, deep in my *heart, I knew I'd never make it to 30 days. I knew you'd never need to file for a divorce. I knew you'd never need to leave our home. Because I knew I would be gone before those 30 days ended, and it would solve the problem. While I considered how to stop you leaving our family, I realised that I needed to ensure I could spend as much time with you as possible; I knew my time was precious, and I wanted it to be with you all.*

I'm not melancholy or even remorseful. I am simply full of regret. Regret that I couldn't be the person you needed me to be, I couldn't be the momma our two monsters deserve. I feel that I have let you all down, and for that I'm truly sorry. I'm sorry I'm not able to be with you as you walk through this wondrous thing called life. I'm sorry I'm not able to watch the kids become the people they are meant to be. I'm sorry I couldn't be the wife you were always meant to have.

If I had a choice, of course, I wouldn't want to divorce you or leave you. I love you. I always have loved you and I always will. But I'd like to think that I'm not a selfish person, and if my choices were making you in any way unhappy I would never stand in your way.

I have said goodbye to the kids individually over the past few days. I have also written each of them a letter that's inside this big envelope. There is also a big box in the bottom of my wardrobe that has letters and cards for each of them for important moments in their lives. In the bottom of our main wardrobe you will find two big boxes containing wrapped presents for all of you from me, again for important moments in your and their lives. I may not be able to be there in person, but everyone should have a present from their momma on their 18th birthday.

Mum, Dad and Andy know that I'm sick. I'm not sure they understand the ins and outs of it, but they know I won't be around for much longer, and without even taking a breath they told me that they will be there for you, in whatever way you need them to be. You will not be on your own.

Please don't be mad at them. They have abided by my wishes that you three were not to know.

I have had a happy life, Lawson. Our life together has been everything I'd hoped when I envisioned being married as a little girl. We created two amazing little mess-creators, and I'm so proud of you all. So proud to call you my life.

My biggest regret about leaving is that I have to leave without making you happy, Lawson. I made a vow, a promise to make you happy for the rest of your life – a colourful marriage – and I haven't and I'm truly sorry, but please know how truly happy you made me.

Love always,
Your Ann

I also found the strength to write the letter for Zak as I was on a bit of a roll. He's going to be invaluable to Lawson when the time comes.

Dear Zak,

First things first, bring beer! He'll need beer.

Secondly, I'm sorry I'm not there to share said beer with you guys.

So my time is done, and I've shuffled off. Possibly to float on a cloud somewhere! JOKE! Nothing like breaking the tension with a good death joke!

Ok serious faces now...

My time has come to an end, and now I need you. For the past...years (more than I'd like to commit to paper) you have been like another brother to me. You've listened to me moan about Lawson, you've moaned about Lawson to me. You've made the best godfather to our two terrors. You made an excellent bedfellow during that camping trip to Lyme Regis (take that look of horror off your face, Lawson – he simply shared the tent with me when you were too drunk to be trusted inside the canvas!).

I need you to love him hard. Catch him when he falls. Shove him when he stumbles. Be practical you, and help organise him in the coming days. Mostly I just need you to be wonderful, amazing, caring, compassionate, kind and generous you.

I will miss all of you terribly. But please know what a wonderful life I have led, and how truly blessed I have been to have you all fill it with colour and magic.

Annie xxx

PS you're going to need my diary – it's in the top drawer of my bedside table. It contains passwords to all my accounts. It also has all the numbers and addresses of my friends. My phone – I'm not sure where exactly it will be when the time comes, but my password is our anniversary 2310. Lawson will be useless at telling people, this is where he'll need you.

Thank you for being one of my most treasured friends, thank you for being Lawson's best friend. I love you.

Annie

~

Dr Pacey came right on time and he brought a colleague from The Tulip Hospice.

It was too much. Unfortunately, I spent most of our time together in tears.

They were both so nice to me – utter arseholes! Stop being so bloody nice to me!

I was, and am, thankful to Dr Pacey for everything that he

has done professionally and personally, but for the love of God!

Stop being so flipping nice!

~

This evening has been the hardest yet. The cramping has increased; the bleeding is heavier.

Lawson was home for dinner and commented that he thought I was a 'little peaky'. Thankfully, he knows I'm tired, so I just put it down to that.

Overall, today has been my most productive and worst day.

Friday 06 May

I have a confession…

I spent most of last night on my phone…

I have been reading up on the 'lead-up to death'…

It could probably be my specialist subject…

"Welcome to tonight's show. Annie Lawson from Worcestershire, your specialist subject is the lead-up to one's death."

You'd have thought there would be loads of information on the subject. However, most of it is a conjecture, hypothesis. The other half is witness testimony of family members witnessing the passing of their loved ones, even near-death experiences.

The consensus, however, remains the same – that there is often a peak in physical and mental health around twenty-four hours before the end.

Although I don't want to tempt fate, I've woken this morning feeling…good.

The kids got off to school ok this morning; thankfully the reluctance of yesterday has gone.

I spoke to Mum on the way home and she asked if the kids could have a sleepover with them tomorrow. So I've packed their cases and left them in the hall where they can see them when they get home tonight; they'll be beside themselves when they see the cases.

My energy levels have been good today, so I made fairy cakes for everyone, and picnic food for dinner.

~

Dr Pacey didn't stay long.

I'm not afraid, I'm not, and I told him that.

I'm just sad to be leaving.

When Lawson left for work this morning I whispered, "I love you" – just in case.

He was home in time for dinner, and we had a fab time having our picnic and of course the fairy cakes!

In the back of this book, I've made lists of everything I can think of.

Lists for when the kids ask:

What was Mommy's favourite…?

What did Mommy say when…?

~

I'm sitting in bed; Lawson is snoring next to me.

I'm reflecting on my life – the good, bad and the downright amazing life I've had.

Life's wonderful moments:

Brixham harbour crabbing.

Fish and chips in paper in the back of Dad's car.

Cinema trips.

Barbecues with the neighbours.

Meeting Lawson.

Dating Lawson.

Our best date? The first picnic in the park.

Our engagement.

Our wedding.

Bringing home Beau.

Our honeymoon in Watermouth.

Pregnant with Lexie.

Moving into the house.

Lexie being born.

Blurriness that was the first few months after Lex came along.

Lexie learning to walk and talk.

Pregnant with Louis.

Louis's birth.

Nothing quite so worrying with Louis as it was with Lex.

Anniversaries.

Birthdays.

Holidays.

Christmases.

My life had been embroidered with a tapestry of beautiful colours thanks to my wonderful Lawson, Lexie, Louis, Andy, Mum and Dad, Janey and even Beau!

Saturday 07 May

I've not slept well; the pain is intense.

I feel that perhaps all those stories may be right, a bit of a revival then bye-bye.

I think I'm as ready now as I'll ever be…

I've made my peace with my guilt about leaving everyone, everything I can is sorted, everyone I need to say goodbye to. I have said I love them.

I know that I'm leaving people who are treasured and loved.

I will leave them knowing that their lives are intertwined with happiness, love, magic, and colour just like they have all given me.

I'm tired.

I'm going to have a nap now and hopefully I will feel better by the time Lawson gets home.

Sunday 08 May

Monday 09 May

Tuesday 10 May

Wednesday 11 May

Mommy's List of Randomness

Colour	Lilac
Smell	My babies' hair
Food	Roast dinner
Scent	Freshly mown grass
Drink	Nice cuppa tea
TV show	Anything that my babies like watching
Book	My first nursery rhymes
Feeling	Being in the middle of a big hug with my babies
Place	Watermouth
Season	Autumn
Clothing	Woolly Pully
Place to sit	In the garden and listen to the birds
Crisps	Ready salted
Chocolate/sweets	Milk chocolate
Holiday	Our first as a family of four
Ways to spend a day	With my wonderful family
Day	Three – marrying Daddy, Lexie being born, Louis being born
Best memory	Our little family being snuggled together

What did Mommy say…?

…when was I born?

"She's the most beautiful baby I've ever seen." Lexie

"He looks like an angel." Louis

…when she tucked us into bed?

"I love you, baby."

"How much?"

"More than is possible and then a bit more."

Lawson,

A final message from me.

   Now you know the whole truth – gore and all.

   I hope you don't think any less of me.

   I tried to do what I thought was best.

   I've spent most of the last few months feeling completely torn as to what was the right thing to do. I'm still not sure if I made the right decision, but it cannot be undone now. Hopefully, I haven't left you with many unanswered questions.

   When the time is right, and if you feel it's the right thing to do, please allow Lexie and Louis to read this journal. Hopefully it will help them understand their old mum!

   I've also written final letters to Mum, Dad, Andy, and your mum – please will you show them?

   Now, my love, the time has come to grieve, and you must! DO NOT deny yourself the time and opportunity to feel the grief.

   However, Lawson, time will pass and slowly you will begin to see colour again.

   I want you to be happy, my love.

   Allow yourself to feel and be embraced with the magic of love again. You deserve to smile. One day in the future, someone will walk into your life and bring fresh air, confidence, and light. Allow them to bring light into your shadows, allow them to love you. Allow yourself to love again.

Always and All-ways,
Forever Your
Ann
xxxx

Janey,

The best mother-in-law I could ask for. My life with Lawson has been so much more enjoyable thanks to your support, advice, kindness, compassion, and tips on how to deal with your boy!

Thank you for everything that you have done for me over the years. I know that Lexie and Louis will grow up in your image to be amazing little humans.

I still remember the first time we met. You had to come and rescue us as Lawson's car had broken down!

"You absolute idiot, Robert! Your dad told you to check the oil before you left!" You raised your voice at him. "Oh, Annie dear, it's so lovely to finally meet you." You embraced me in a hug. "Here's your oil, idiot," you said, dumping the bottle on the floor in front of Lawson. "Come on, Annie, you and I are going to the pub!" you added, as you ushered me into your nice warm car.

Lawson will eventually be ok, I'm sure of that. However, I suspect he will struggle with some of the basics of being a mum and dad rolled into one. Perhaps some lessons on helping with Lexie's hairstyles as she gets older?

The grandmother you have become is truly something to behold. You are wonderful and the children worship the ground you walk on. Thank you from the bottom of my heart for being so bloomin' amazing.

Time to say goodbye now, my darling Janey. Please know how dearly I cherish you.

I love you.

Your
Annie
xxxx

Mum and Dad,

So where do I begin?

How about – chipppppppers…!

Thank you for so many things.

For being my first friends, first taxis, teachers, safety blanket, instructors, my port within any storm, binge-watching film companions – my world.

From the moment I was born, you have wrapped me tightly within your arms and pushed me to always achieve my dreams.

I truly lucked out on the parent front! Most of my friends while I was growing up were always angry or annoyed with their parents. I don't think I've ever felt like that, ever. You've been firm but fair to both me and Andy. I hope this is something I've replicated with Lexie and Louis.

Aww, our baby mess makers! What amazing role models they have in you! Becoming a parent has always been a goal for me. However, watching you two and the life job you had being parents to me, and Andy, change with the birth of Lexie was…mesmerising. You've both matured and grown into this newfound role and it was the making of you.

Never once, even for a second, since becoming a parent, did I feel alone, or that Lawson and I would have to find our way in the messy haziness that is the days that come after a baby is born.

I love you both dearly and leaving you both will be so hard, but I know my leaving is all the easier because I've lived a full and glorious life.

Forever and always,
Your Annie Bear
xxxx

Squidge,

Head up, you old sod!

Come on now, no point getting yourself all upset and showing everyone your snotty face!

My wonderful big bro'. Oh, how I love you. I really am so lucky to have you as my guide throughout life. You've always been there to show me the right way (sometimes the wrong way) but mostly how to enjoy and embrace life. I couldn't have asked for a better brother than you.

Thank you for so many things that I do not have enough pages left in this book, but the things that stick in my mind:

– The most ridiculous carrot slippers for Christmas!

– Melting marshmallows on our first solo camping trip in the back garden!

– Me overseeing the pressing of 'record' on the tape as we listened to the Top 40 – so many nerves!

– That swing and slide set we got for Christmas – it was epic, wasn't it?

– Going to the cinema and spilling the popcorn all over the floor, and moving seats so no one will know it was us!

– Singing Christmas carols for Nan and Gramp – even if you were a bit off-key!

– Going out in your car for the first time after you passed your test – so flipping scared!

– Being your best man/woman. Even though your marriage didn't last, I was so honoured to stand next to you.

Simply being your sister, it's been a fantastic journey and I LOVE YOU!

Be brave, my wonderful Squidge. Remember to look for the pot of gold at the end of the rainbow, because one day you will find it!

All my love for you always and a bit more,
Mouse
xxxxxx

Message from Fi

Thank you so much for taking the time to read Rob and Annie's stories.

I hope you've had as much fun reading them as I have writing them.

Lawson and Annie had been living with me for a good few years before I began putting pen to paper.

Initially, when I began to write The Colour of Marriage, I only ever intended for it to be a single novel. However, there came a specific point in the story when I realised that Annie's story needed to be told.

For those who've read The Colour of Marriage, it's when Lawson takes the book down to the harbour, sits down in the sunshine and begins to read Annie's words.

My overriding hope and wish for both books is that Lawson, Annie and I are able to reinforce the overarching belief that every minute of your life matters, you matter and you are important.

So from all of us (including the sock-stealing Beau) thank you for taking this journey with us.

Fi

xx

The Colour of Marriage

Read the first book of The Colour of Marriage *series*
by Fiona Partridge

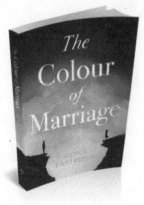

Life has a way of showing us what is really important. But what if you get it wrong? Only then do you realise you were in the right place all along.

When fate decides there is no tomorrow, no second chances, no way back, how can you bring the light back into your life and face an unknown future?

Rob Lawson was part of something truly remarkable.

Will he be able to recognise that before it's too late and hold on to the colour of marriage?

ISBN 978-1-80042-108-0 (paperback)
ISBN 978-1-80042-109-7 (ebook)
Bookseller and library discounts available
Published by SilverWood Books

Lightning Source UK Ltd.
Milton Keynes UK
UKHW041929290422
402296UK00012B/151

9 781800 422056